George Manville Fenn

The Sapphire Cross

Vol. II

George Manville Fenn

The Sapphire Cross
Vol. II

ISBN/EAN: 9783337066376

Printed in Europe, USA, Canada, Australia, Japan

Cover: Foto ©Andreas Hilbeck / pixelio.de

More available books at **www.hansebooks.com**

THE SAPPHIRE CROSS.

A Novel.

BY

G. MANVILLE FENN.

IN THREE VOLUMES.
VOL. II.

LONDON:
TINSLEY BROTHERS, 18, CATHERINE ST., STRAND.
1871.

JOHN CHILDS AND SON, PRINTERS.

CONTENTS OF VOL. II.

BOOK II.—SECOND GENERATION.

THE SAPPHIRE CROSS.

CHAPTER XXVI.

NOCTURNAL.

'PERHAPS, after all, it's just as weel that he did not come,' mused Alexander M'Cray, as he stood one morning upon the long wooden bridge which connected, at the narrowest part, the two shores of the fine piece of water lying between the park of Merland Castle and the pleasure-grounds. He was leaning over the rail, and gazing down into the clear depths below, where, screened by the broad leaves of the water-lilies, which here and there bore some sweet white chalice, the huge carp were floating lazily, now and then giving a flip with their broad tails to send themselves a few feet through the limpid medium in which they dwelt.

'Perhaps, after all, it's just as weel that he did not come any more, but if he had, I would have pitched him in here as freely as have look-ed at him, and he wouldn't have hurt neither —a bad chiel. Them that's born to be hanged will never be drowned, and he'll come to the gallows sure enough, and deserves it, too, for ill-using that poor bairn as he did.'

'Weel, this winna do,' he said, starting from his reverie, and shouldering the broom with which he had been sweeping the bridge. 'I'll just e'en go and do the paths under the bedroom windows ; the lassie might happen to give a look out.'

The gardener walked on, thoughtfully gazing up at the windows, and thinking the while of the nights when he had watchfully made his way, stealthy as a burglar, from bush to bush, or crouched beneath the shrubs. Few nights had passed without his seeing Jane Barker's light extinguished, but there had been no further visit from John Gurdon.

'He didn't like the flat of my spade,' said M'Cray, with a grin, and this seemed to be the case—the ex-butler never from that night having been heard of. Still, more now from habit than anything, the gardener continued his nocturnal rounds, telling himself that he could not sleep without one peep at the lassie's window before going to bed.

But Alexander M'Cray seemed to make but little progress in his love affairs. Whenever he met Jane she had always a pleasant smile for him, but he knew in his heart that it was not the smile he wished to see.

'But bide a wee,' he said. 'Her puir heart's sair. Wait awhile and it will all come reet.'

The gardener was favoured that morning, for as he applied his broom lightly here and there to the wandering leaves, the early ones of autumn, he heard a window, above his head, thrown open, and as he looked up, there was Jane leaning out, ready to smile and nod down to him.

'Company coming, lassie?' said M'Cray, leaning upon his broom.

'Company? No, Mr M'Cray,' said Jane; 'why did you think so?'

'Because ye're getting ready the best bed-room,' said the gardener.

'Oh dear, no,' said Jane; 'we shall never have company here again, I think. I'm only having this put ready for Sir Murray himself, because some of the old plaster ceiling of his own room's come down.'

'Puir lad! he looks bad,' said M'Cray.

'And serve him right, too,' said Jane, defiantly. 'I haven't patience with him.'

'Nay, lassie, perhaps not,' said M'Cray. 'But ye've plenty of patience with them as is waur.'

'Please don't talk about that,' said Jane, pleadingly.

'Nay, lassie, then I winna,' said M'Cray, sadly; 'but be patient mysel', if it's for twenty long years ere ye turn to me.'

Jane leaned out, giving the gardener one long earnest gaze, such a one as made his heart beat more freely, but the coming steps of some one along a neighbouring path sent Jane to her work, and M'Cray's broom rustling over gravel and leaf.

Before many seconds had passed Lady

Gernon came by, very pale and thoughtful. She had a basket in her hand, and, evidently bent upon some expedition, she made her way through the ring fence, and away across the park, neither looking to the right nor left.

'Siller and titles are nice things,' mused M'Cray; 'but they don't seem to make yon puir creature happy.'

M'Cray swept as he thought, and thought as he swept. Jane did not again appear at the window, and if she had done so, the opening of one in the lower range would have kept him from speaking to her, while, as he swept on and on, hunting out errant leaves from the hiding-places where they were waiting for a bit of fun with the wind, he became conscious of the dark, lowering face of Sir Murray, apparently watching the progress of his lady from the side of the house where he now was.

'He's a puir, miserable sort of chiel,' muttered the gardener; 'he seems to want a rousing up. It's my belief that a few hours' trenching a day wi' a good broad spade wad do him a world of good. He eats too much, and he drinks too much; but I'm sorry for him, puir lad—I'm sorry for him!'

That night Alexander M'Cray sat in his little room, thoroughly enjoying himself, for he was so elated with the glance Jane had that morning bestowed upon him, that he had treated himself to a pipe and a small tumbler of whisky and water, over which he sat smiling and happy, for it struck him that he had at last got in the thin edge of the wedge, and that the future would all be plain sailing.

'And she's as good a woman as ever the sun shone on,' said Sandy at last, as, after draining the last drop from his tumbler of whisky and water, and trying in vain to ignite the ashes at the bottom of his pipe, he tapped the bowl upon the bar, and then stood up to think.

Should he?—shouldn't he? The night was dark and gusty, and he had sat thinking till it was long past twelve. There was nothing to go for, and the lassie's light might be out, and she fast asleep in bed long enough before; but then he would have the satisfaction of knowing that all was right, and for months past now he had not missed a night. He did not think he would go, though, for it was evident now that Jane was beginning to think a little of his words, and no doubt matters would soon brighten up and be settled. No, he would not go to-night—there was no need; and upon the strength of that resolution he took off his coat, and methodically hung it behind the door. Then out came his snuff-box, when a pinch or two seemed to drive away the happy ease engendered by the whisky and water, clearing his brain, and forcing him to think of the realities of life.

'No,' he thought now, 'it would not be right to give up what he had taught himself was a duty. How did he know but what, after all, that John Gurdon might come back that very night, and put back in a few moments what it had taken him months to erase?'

'I'll go,' said Sandy, 'if it's only for the name of the thing. I mean to win the lassie if leaving no stone unturned will do it; and now, here's a little wee bit of crag lying in my way, and I'm too idle to touch it. Sandy M'Cray, take your cap, mon, and go and do your duty. It's the little tiny cracks that open out into big splits, so stop them up when they're small. Keep your trees pruned back, my lad, or they'll grow wild and ragged; and whenever ye feel a weed coming up in your nature, pull him up direct. This bit of wanting to stop away is a weed, lad, so pull it up at once.'

Sandy M'Cray must have taken it out by the very roots, for the next minute he had closed his door, and was stealthily walking over the grass towards the pleasure-grounds.

There was not a step of the way that was not familiar, and on the darkest night he could have avoided every flower-bed, as if by instinct, or even have made his way blindfold; hence he had soon crossed the bridge, and walked softly on towards the great lawn, noting, as he went, that there was not a single light visible in the great mansion.

'I'll just go the length of the place, and then stop for a moment by the lassie's window, and home again,' muttered M'Cray, and then he stopped short, for a hand was laid upon his shoulder, and a voice whispered in his ear :

'Stay here a few minutes, Joe. He's gone to have a look up at the back windows, and I'll go this side. Don't move, because it's so confoundedly dark!'

M'Cray felt the next minute, rather than saw, that he was alone. His breath came thickly, and his heart beat fast, as, wiping the sweat from his forehead, he bent down and ran softly over the grass to the edge of the lawn, leaped the gravel walk so as to land upon the other side, and then, softly creeping amongst the bushes, he hurried towards where Jane's window looked down, a strange beating at his temples, and an aching void at his heart.

'And only to think,' he muttered, 'me sitting drinking mysel' drunk, and all the while the spoiler coming after my little ewe lamb.'

But Sandy's spirits rose as he cautiously

crept up, to find that Jane's window was
closed; he could just distinguish that from
the faint glimmering of the glass. The rob-
bers would gain no entrance, then, there;
upon that point he could feel happy, and,
with a weight removed from his mind, he
stood thinking of what he should do.

He did not for a moment entertain a
doubt but that it was Gurdon and his friends
come back at last, perhaps ready to force an
entrance, and open to murder as well as to
rob. But Sandy's heart was glad within him
—his lassie was free of all complicity; and if
they got at her now, it should only be over
his strong body. But he felt that there
was no fear of Jane being again deceived; the
last occasion had been too plain an unveil-
ing of John Gurdon's character; so, hastily
making up his mind as to his proceedings, he
crept from amongst the bushes on his hands

and knees, and set himself to try and discover where the nocturnal visitors now were, previously to taking further steps to baffle their plot.

The gardener had not long to seek, for before he had advanced far, a faint whispering told him where the enemy lay, while at the same moment the snap of a fastening and the gliding up of a window told him that an entrance had been effected.

14

CHAPTER XXVII.

THE BURGLARY.

'THE de'ils ha' been quick about it,' muttered Sandy; 'and they've gone through
the libr'y window, while, if that door I broke
open has been mended again, it's a strange
thing to me. What shall I do?—ring them
all up? No,' he said, after a pause; 'then perhaps we shouldn't catch them, for before I
could get round again from the bell, they'd
have slipped out of the window. No, we must
catch them, for it strikes me verra strongly
that if this is Mr Jock Gurdon, I should like

to see him transported to the other side of the watter.'

For a few moments Sandy M'Cray stood thoughtful and puzzling what to do. He could easily have alarmed the burglars, for such they evidently were; but then that was not sufficient—there must be a capture made. But suddenly a bright thought struck him—he would run round to the butler's pantry, and try and rouse whoever slept there. But did any one sleep there? Gurdon's place had never been filled up, and it was most likely that the footman and under-butler still kept their places in the hall.

' I have it,' muttered Sandy, at last; and setting off across the lawn at a brisk trot, he made his way to the kitchen garden, but what he sought was not there, of course not : it was round by the potting shed, he recollected then; and on cautiously proceeding there, he picked up from where it lay beside a wall a twenty-round light garden ladder, and set off with it to the front of the house, where he had spoken to Jane that morning.

'One—two—three—four; that's the window,' muttered Sandy, and the next instant, exerting his great strength, he raised the ladder and rested the top against the window sill.

Fortunately, the window entered so quickly by the burglars was on the other side of the house, and the gardener was able to take his steps for giving an alarm unheard by them.

'Gude save us!' he muttered, climbing up. 'I hope he winna shute me!'

The next minute he listened attentively, and then gave three sharp taps upon one pane, followed by two other similar signals, ere the blind was dragged back, the window thrown open, and Sir Murray's hands were tightly grasping his throat.

'Hoot awa', Sir Mooray, and tak' awa' ye're hands from a man's weam.'

'Hand over the letter, you scoundrel, or I'll hurl you down!' exclaimed Sir Murray, through his teeth.

'The chiel's been sleeping in his clothes, and gone half daft,' muttered Sandy. And then, in a whisper: 'Let me in, Sir Mooray, and look sharp, for there are burglars in the house!'

The gardener's announcement seemed to bring his master to his right senses, and, loosing his hold, Sandy stepped lightly into the chamber.

'You'll just have a pair of pistols, or dirk, or something, Sir Mooray,' said the man.

His master stepped to a drawer, and drew

out a small double-barrelled pair, examined the nipples to see if they were capped, and then handed one to his servant, but the latter shook his head.

'Na—na,' he said; 'I might be blowing his brains out with the thing, and I dinna wush that. I'll take the poker, Sir Mooray; and now, if ye're ready, the sooner we're at them the better.'

'Ring the alarm-bell!' said Murray.

'Nay, nay, gude sir; let's take them ourselves. Stop the hole up where they come in, and then we can ring if ye like; but while we're ringing bells they'll be off, and only to come again.'

Giving up the leadership to his servant, Sir Murray followed him into the corridor, and from thence to the grand staircase, but all was still. Hastily descending to the library, the unrepaired door was found—like the window

—wide open, when Sandy's first step was to close both carefully, and then rejoin his master.

' Heard anything, sir? ' he whispered.

' Not a sound,' said Sir Murray, hoarsely; ' but, do you think they are burglars? Stay here an instant, while I ascend to her ladyship's room,' he said, hurriedly, as a thought —a base, suspicious thought of a meditated elopement—crossed his mind. ' They may have gone that way.'

' Hoot, mon, stay where ye are,' whispered Sandy. 'D'ye hear that? They're packing up the plate, and—hist! look there,' he said, in a low tone, as a faint light shone in the distance on their right, making plain the face of a man standing in the second of the suite of drawing-rooms, the doors of which had been set wide open.

Sandy recognized the face at the same instant as Sir Murray, and the same name rose to their lips, M'Cray muttering fiercely :

'Stop ye here, Sir Mooray, and lay hold of the de'ils taking the plate. They winna face yer pistols. I'll deal with this one.'

Thrusting his master aside, M'Cray stepped lightly over the soft carpets, followed for a few seconds by the baronet's eyes, but the light then faded away, and as Sir Murray stood, now breathing hard and excited, as he felt that it was indeed a burglary in progress, he heard a muttered oath, the crashing over of a set of fire-irons, the heavy sounds of blows, and knocking down of furniture, followed directly after by a rapid rush, and he felt himself dashed to the ground, one pistol exploding as he fell; but he was up again the next moment, to be knocked down with greater violence than before, as a Scotch oath rang in his ear; and then, at the same instant, there was a crash and splintering of glass, and as he rose to his feet, he became aware that those who had knocked him down had gone through the library and leapt boldly through the closed window, the night wind now coming with a loud sigh through the shivered panes.

' The scoundrel has escaped, and the other gone in pursuit,' muttered Sir Murray, just as loud shrieks for help were heard from above-stairs, followed by the loud ringing of the alarm-bell.

The next minute lights were held over the balustrade, and timid faces were seen, gazing down; but the lights also revealed to Sir Murray's gaze the crape-veiled features of two men, each bearing a bag, which now, upon finding that they were discovered, they dropped, with a loud, jingling noise, upon the stone floor—a sound which told plainly enough of their contents.

' Stand ! ' cried Sir Murray, as they

turned to flee down the long passage up
which they had come—a passage leading to
the pantry—' stand, or I fire ! I cannot miss
you at this distance ! '

One of the men uttered an oath, in his
rage, for now a light appeared at the other
end of the passage, showing a footman, armed
with a blunderbuss, which seemed to alarm
him as much as it did the burglars.

' It's no go,' muttered one of the men.
' Stow that, gov'nor, and I'll give up. Come
on, Joe.'

' Not I,' exclaimed the other, making a
spring to get by Sir Murray, but in vain :
true to his word, the baronet fired, and with a
shriek of agony, the man sprang into the air,
and then fell heavily upon the stone floor,
which was soon stained with his blood.

' Why didn't you give up, then, like a
man ? ' whined his sympathizing companion,

who was now hastily secured by two of the men-servants. 'The gent wouldn't have hurt yer, if yer had only give up when he arst. There, don't pull a cove about like that, and yer needn't tie so tight. I ain't agoin' to run away so as to get shot, I can tell you.'

'Lift the other up,' said Sir Murray, hoarsely; when the man was found to be bleeding profusely, though evidently not wounded in a vital spot.

'You are not hurt, Murray?' whispered a voice at his ear just then, and the baronet turned to find Lady Gernon anxiously scanning his face.

'No; not dead yet,' he said, brutally. 'Go to your own room.'

Lady Gernon turned away with a weary sigh, and Sir Murray stood guard over his prisoners, when a shudder of terror ran through the party assembled; for, faintly heard, apparently from somewhere in the grounds, came what sounded like a wild appeal for help.

CHAPTER XXVIII.

A RIVAL EMBRACE.

SIR MURRAY GERNON was right in his surmise, for when M'Cray, eager to secure the person of his supposed rival, hurried across the drawing-room, and in the darkness made a bound to where he had seen the lighted match fade out, his enemy had made a slight movement, so that he failed to obtain a good hold ; and in the brief struggle which ensued close to the fireplace, M'Cray was thrown heavily upon the floor, and his adversary dashed through the drawing-room out into

the hall, striking down Sir Murray in his
effort to reach the library.   But M'Cray was
after him directly, and had no hesitation in
leaving his master where he, too, had knocked
him down ; while, following the burglar's ex-
ample, he leaped, in his excitement, right
through the broken window.

'Oh, my best pelargoniums ! ' groaned
the gardener, as he picked himself up, after
coming down crash into a flower-bed beneath
the window.   ' Ye shall pay for this, though,
Maister Gurdon, or my name's not Sandy
M'Cray ! '   And then, favoured by a break in
the clouds, he caught sight of Gurdon running rapidly towards the bridge.

'Ye'll not get there first, laddie,' muttered the Scot, as, exerting all his powers, he
dashed over the lawn, to cut off his quarry's
retreat in that direction; and being the
lustier man of the two, he soon had the satis-

faction of seeing his foe double, and run along the brink of the lake, as if to get round the house; for it was growing each moment lighter, the wind springing up, and sweeping the heavy curtain of clouds from the face of the heavens.

'If ye think I canna rin ye doon, Jock Gurdon,' muttered M'Cray, 'ye're making a meestake. I'll have ye, if I rin for a week!'

He pressed on, gaining so fast upon the burglar, that he once more doubled, and dodging round a thick plantation of shrubs, M'Cray was, for a minute, thrown off the scent; but his shrewd Scottish nature stood him in good stead.

'He'll make again for the bridge,' he thought; and with a grim smile of determination upon his face, he ran in that direction; but, to his great disappointment, he seemed to be at fault, for there was no sign anywhere of the fugitive. But, for all that, Sandy's idea was correct, as he found, after harking backwards and forwards two or three times. Gurdon—for it was indeed he who had, with his companions, attempted the burglary—had been making his way for the bridge, when his ear, sharpened by fright, told him that his enemy was coming in the same direction, and he directly crouched amidst a bed of laurels, to wait, panting, for an opportunity to escape. He knew that transportation must be his fate if taken; and that if, in revenge, he said anything respecting the character of Lady Gernon, it would merely be taken as the calumny of a discharged servant. No, he thought, he must not be taken—he could not afford yet to give up his liberty.

His breath came more freely at the end of a minute, for his heart had been labouring heavily. Wasted by drink and debauchery, he was in no training for such violent effort; and he was beginning to hope that an opportunity might yet offer for his reaching the bridge, and escaping through the park—the other way by the village he dared not try—when, with a rush, M'Cray came right through the thicket where he crouched; and, like a hare roused from its form, away he darted, and the pursuit commenced anew.

There was no hiding now: there was too much light, and pursuer and pursued were too close together. Making almost frantic efforts to get away, after dodging and doubling again and again, to the great injury of M'Cray's long legs, which, when at speed, carried him again and again past his foe, Gurdon made a feint or two and then dashed fiercely for the bridge once more.

' If I'd only got one of those powdered loons to stop his gait there,' muttered M'Cray;

and he made a furious effort, nearly catching
his prey, and completely cutting off his retreat,
for as the Scot shot by him, Gurdon doubled
again, and ran along the lake, but only for a
little way. There was a bend there, and the
water was on both sides of him as he ran along
the tongue of land : he must either face his
enemy in another rush for the bridge, or take
to the black water, gleaming below him.

But Gurdon had, to his cost, always been
a hater of the limpid element, and, turning
now like a beast at bay, he dashed, with
clenched fists, at the gardener, intending to
fell him, and then rush on for liberty. But he
did not know his man : as he came down,
with a fierce charge, M'Cray merely leaned
a little on one side so as to avoid the
blow, and the next instant his arms were
wreathed tightly round the ex-butler's body,
and the two were struggling furiously upon

the turf, rolling over and over, their muttered ejaculations and execrations mingling in a fierce growl as of two savage beasts of prey.

'Ah! would ye?' exclaimed M'Cray, at last. 'Ye murderous-minded villin, would ye use a knife? Take that—and that, and— Save us, we shall be—'

M'Cray's ejaculation was suddenly brought to an end, for in the fierce struggle made for the possession of the knife Gurdon had managed to draw and open, at a time when the gardener thought him about to succumb, they had, unnoticed, drawn nearer and nearer to the edge of the lake, and, perhaps to the saving then of the Scotchman's life, suddenly plunged together into one of the deepest parts.

Gurdon dropped the knife as he rose to the surface, and, loosing his grasp of his pursuer, he struggled furiously to reach the bank; but M'Cray's northern blood was up to a heat

so fierce, that the water seemed only to make
it hiss furiously instead of quenching his
ardour, and he held on to his adversary like a
bull-dog, when, with the fear of drowning
before him, Gurdon uttered the wild appealing
cry for help that had been heard at the
Castle, and turned once more to struggle with
his foe.

Once again only, as his head was above
water, did Gurdon shriek, giving utterance to
a yell of horror that was hardly human, for
the feeling was strong upon him now, as they
struggled farther and farther from the shore,
that the gardener was trying to drown him.
But no such thought was in M'Cray's breast:
his determination was to make a capture, and,
unlike his enemy, a capital swimmer, the
water had no terrors for him. Every one of
Gurdon's efforts was interpreted to mean
escape, and, heedless of the peril and suffoca-

tion, the struggle was continued, the water being lashed into foam, till, at last, M'Cray, as they rose to the surface after a long immersion, awoke to the fact that his quarry was nearly exhausted, and that they were in deadly peril; for Gurdon's arms were clutched round him in a deadly grip that there was no undoing. They were far from the bank, and, in the rapid glance he took around, he knew that they were in about twelve feet of water.

'There'll be something for the big pike to go at, if it does come to it,' thought M'Cray, with a grim feeling of despair; 'but, anyhow, he'll trouble the puir lassie nae mair.'

The water, bubbling round his lips, checked M'Cray's thoughts for a few moments, or rather gave them a new direction; but rising once more to the surface, with one arm at liberty, he struck out fiercely, to keep himself afloat.

'If I could get to the bridge-piles!' he thought, as through the darkness he could dimly make out the little green, slimy pier, not many yards from him. 'Gude help me! I dinna want to die yet!'

He fought on for his life, beating the strangling water from his lips, and tearing furiously to reach the pile, where, perhaps, he might be able to hold on till help came. Once, through the darkness, he heard voices, and caught a glimpse of a light dancing about; but the next moment the water was thundering in his ears, and its blackness seemed to blot out all vision.

Another few moments of strangling horror, and he had once more fought his way to the surface; but he was yards away from the bridge-piles, and a feeling now of despair came upon him, dulling his tired faculties, and seeming to warn him that all was over. There was no help that he could see near at hand, for the servants with Sir Murray Gernon did not seem to know which direction to take. It seemed so hard, too, just as he had begun to feel hopeful about his love, to be dragged down by their common enemy to the depths of the lake; and at last, as he felt the water closing over him, he gave another fierce struggle, forcing himself up an instant, till he had uttered the hoarse, harsh, despairing cry of a dying man—dying in the hour of his full strength—and then there were a few bubbles and rings upon the surface of the water, where, locked still in their deadly embrace, the rivals had gone down.

CHAPTER XXIX.

THE HELPING HAND.

MRS NORTON had gone to her rest that night in tears, for her husband had been absent for some days. His restlessness seemed of late to have been largely on the increase, so that when he was at home she was kept upon a tremble of expectation lest at any time he might be gone. True, he was always quiet and gentle, and proud as ever of his boy; but the proximity of the Gernons was like a cloud over him, and as she determinedly drove away the suspicions that would try to fasten upon her, Ada Norton could not but own to herself that while the Gernons were at the Castle, or they themselves stayed at the Hall, there could be no real happiness for her. She knew well enough how it preyed upon her husband's spirits, when, from time to time, rumours of the state of affairs reached them. She had hoped that a reconciliation would long ere this have taken place—that is to say, between husband and wife ; but the fact of their complete estrangement, taken in connection with Sir Murray's character, and Captain Norton's strange, reserved behaviour, always seemed to be the hold by which doubt tried again and again to fasten upon her.

Philip Norton came not that night, and Mrs Norton lay weakly weeping, determined in her own mind that, in spite of their poverty, she would try and persuade him to leave the Hall—to go anywhere, so that they might but keep together. She knew that, on account of his connection with the mines, it would be useless to endeavour to get him to move to a distance ; but even a few miles farther away would, she felt, bring them more peace ; of that she felt assured, telling herself that her husband's frequent absences now were caused by a desire to be away from the place.

But Ada Norton was wrong when, in despair, she gave herself up that night to tears, for her husband was on his way back—at least, he had determined upon sleeping that night at home. He had reached the town rather late, low-spirited and disheartened at the state of his affairs, and had walked towards the primitive inn, meaning to hire a dog-cart and drive over, for months had elapsed since he had sold his own horses, dismissed his groom, and made other reductions in his little establishment. He hired no dog-cart, however, for the state of his finances struck him; and, sturdily preparing himself for the task, he set off to walk the ten miles between him and Merland Hall.

The lonely road seemed well fitted for contemplation, and the thoughts which passed through his breast were many, but none so serious as those which oppressed him when, tired with his long journey, he approached the palings which skirted the park of Merland Castle, stopping at length, in spite of himself, to look over at the nearest point to the house, and gaze long and earnestly at the windows, when suddenly a wild, appealing cry for help smote his ear.

For a moment he paused. Then the cry rang out again, apparently from the direction of the lake—a cry that there was no mistaking, telling, as it did, of a soul in mortal peril; and, heedless of consequence, of the trespass he was committing, and of the relations existing between Sir Murray and himself, he leaped over the palings, and ran in the direction of the sounds.

Naturally his was too generous a spirit to refuse help in need, while now his senses were disturbed by an undefined state of dread, for in some way it seemed that this cry must be connected with Lady Gernon, and once a fearful idea flashed across his mind.

What and if, in utter despair, she had—

He could not finish the thought, but shudderingly dashed on, in a headlong career, till he reached the lake, when he could just make out the splashing and panting in the water.

All was plain enough now : some one was drowning near to the bridge, but more towards the side next the house, while he was in the park.

He would have dashed in upon the instant, but his good sense told him that his plan should be to run along the brink to the bridge, which he did with all the speed he could command, when, divesting himself of coat, vest, and hat, he threw them on the railing, tearing his sleeve, as he hurriedly dragged it off, his every nerve stirred, as from beneath him arose M'Cray's wild and despairing cry. The next instant, though, Norton had climbed the railing, heedless that he swept his garments into the lake, and then, standing upon a portion of the woodwork, he gazed down at the black water for a few moments, striving to make out the centre of the fast-fading rings, before, with a plunge, he cut the air, divided the waters, and disappeared.

In a few moments he was again on the surface, swimming round, and preparing to dive again, feeling that he had come too late, and that in the darkness it was impossible to render aid, when, within a yard of where he was swimming, and seen but for an instant, the fingers and a portion of a clutching hand were visible above the surface, and ere they could sink far, Norton had grasped them in his hand. The next minute he had avoided a dangerous embrace, and was striking out for the nearest point, the slippery piles of the bridge, where, if he could swim so far with his burden, he could, perhaps, hold up the drowning man till assistance came.

It was a hard task, but Norton was a bold and strong swimmer, and before long he was grasping at the slimy woodwork, to slip back again and again; but, at last, he managed to get one arm over a cross-piece, and his legs twined round an upright, while with his disengaged arm he did all that he could under the circumstances—held the heads of the men above water.

To his great joy he now heard voices, and saw a light moving about in the grounds, when, shouting loudly, he saw a hurried movement of the light, and two or three more cries brought the seekers in the right direction.

'Quick, men—quick!' he cried, as some one ran up, and held down the light, while others clustered round on the bank.

'Fetch the boat up,' cried Sir Murray; and his voice sent a thrill through Norton's frame, as he felt that he would have to face him. But he was too much exhausted by his exertions to think much of the threatened encounter. He knew he could hold out but a few minutes longer, and he once more called to them to hasten.

'Who is it? What have you got there?' cried the man with the light.

'Two drowning men,' was the hoarse

reply; 'and I can hold on but a few minutes longer.'

But now came the plash plash of oars, and in a very short time the boat was by the bridge—a small pleasure-boat, into which, with great difficulty, the two men, still tightly locked together, were dragged.

'We can't take you this time very well,' said one of the grooms, who was in the boat.

'Yes—yes,' said another, 'we must manage him somehow.'

'I can wait till you return,' said Norton quietly, for, relieved of his burden, he was able to stretch first one, and then another, cramped limb, and besides, now that he had a little time for thought, the peculiarity of his position struck him. From the scattered words let fall by the servants, he had learned that an attempt had been made to rob the Castle, and that one, if not both the men he had rescued must be connected with the attempt. But, while setting aside as absurd the idea that he could in any way be connected with the matter, he was troubled about the light in which Sir Murray's distempered mind would view his presence in the park at such an hour, and he watched, with no little anxiety, the putting off of the boat.

The man with the lanthorn still kept to the bank, and the bridge remained deserted; so, after a few moments' thought, Philip Norton took a firm hold of one of the cross-pieces of wood, drew himself safely up from the water, and then, all dripping as he was, he climbed the pier till he could reach the railings, and step over. Then, after a little search, he found his hat, but his coat and vest, which he had left hanging upon the rail, were, as we have seen, floating below, upon the surface of the lake.

Meanwhile, his suspicious nature charged, as it were, with so much inflammable matter, ready to blaze up at the contact of the slightest spark, Sir Murray Gernon stood on the bank, waiting the return of the boat. He had heard plainly enough the voice calling for help, and felt sure that he recognized it. Hence, then, he watched eagerly the return of the little skiff, from out of which were lifted the apparently lifeless bodies of M'Cray and Gurdon.

'The villain! I half suspected him,' exclaimed Sir Murray, as he had the lanthorn held down, and recognized in the first the lineaments of his late butler. 'But quick—back, and bring off the other. Who was it, do you know?'

'Couldn't tell, Sir Murray,' said the groom in the boat. 'Seemed to know the voice, too.'

'Back at once, then,' said the baronet, his brow knitting as he tried to solve this new riddle; for if it were, as he so strongly suspected, Captain Norton, what was he doing in the park at that time of night? Lady Gernon had made her appearance, dressed, when there was the alarm in the house.

For a few moments the rush of blood to his head seemed to blind him, and his knees shook, for he fancied that he was about to have another seizure. But he recovered himself in a few moments, and again took up the train of thought. John Gurdon—burglarious entry—Norton apparently in league with him, and ready to try and save his life. What did it all mean? Was Norton a greater scoundrel even than he had given him the credit of being, and was this some new plot for aggrandizing himself at the weak husband's expense? If so, who were mixed up in it?

He staggered again, as the blood flew to his head, in his vain endeavours to piece together the scraps of the puzzle, so as to make a defined whole. But once more, with an effort, he shook off the weakness, and, stooping down, he scooped up some water in the hollow of his hand, and bathed his face, for he was now alone, the servants who had accompanied him having borne the two insensible men to the house.

The next minute the boat returned, and her prow struck the bank.

' Well ? ' said Sir Murray, eagerly, for the men were alone.

' He's gone, sir,' said the groom, solemnly. ' The piles are very slippery, and the poor fellow, whoever he was, could hold on no longer. We've been feeling about with the sculls, but we can't find him.'

Again that rushing of blood to the head

and the choking sensation, and Sir Murray Gernon gasped for air, as he staggered about like a drunken man.

Could it be possible ? Was it Norton, and was he removed from his path ?—removed by his own act while engaged in some nefarious scheme ?

For a few moments a strange sense of mingled exultation and horror oppressed the baronet, and he stood staring vacantly in the faces of his servants.

Would he like them to go and try again ? though, as the water was so deep, there was not much chance of finding the poor fellow till morning.

Yes, he would like them to go; and he would come with them himself; and, entering the boat, Sir Murray made the weary men row on and on, backwards and forwards, through the two openings of the wooden bridge, as, armed himself with the weed-grapnel in the prow, he dragged it over the same ground again and again, expecting at each check it received that it was hooked in the body of the man whom he looked upon as the blight of his existence.

At length, the men being completely worn out, the search was given up till daylight, and Sir Murray returned to the Castle, to find M'Cray sitting up in bed with a blanket round him, sipping whisky and water, hot and strong.

' Gude sake, Sir Mooray ! ' he exclaimed, as his master entered. ' We won the day. I ken a' aboot it—how ye shot one and took the ither; and Jock Gurdon's coming round—the villin !—and no more dead than I am. But it had got verra close to the end, Sir Mooray.'

' My brave fellow ! ' exclaimed his master —' you did nobly.'

'Hoot! just naething at a', Sir Mooray. But winna ye try the whuskee?'

'No, my good fellow. But I don't know how I am to reward you.'

'Hoot! then, Sir Mooray, I'll just tell ye,' said the Scot, whose eye was even now on the main chance. 'Tam Wilkins is a gude servant, but he's auld, and past the gairden. Suppose ye mak' me head gairdener, and give Jenny Barker a hint that she'd better marry me as soon as we've transported Jock Gurdon.'

'My good fellow, I'll stand your friend, depend upon it,' said the baronet, smiling in spite of himself. But the next moment he frowned heavily, as he said, in a low voice: 'Do you know who it was that saved you?'

'No, Sir Mooray, unless it was one of the lads in the bit skiff. But this is rare whuskee, Sir Mooray!'

Sir Murray frowned more deeply before speaking again.

'Did you see any one with the villain you so nobly captured? Though how you came to suspect the attack I don't know.'

'Not a soul; only the two ye've taken, Sir Mooray,' said Sandy, reddening, perhaps from the effect of the whisky. 'And as to suspecting, I have no suspicion in me; but I jist like to see of a night that naebody's after the grapes or bit of wall-fruit, for Tam Wilkins is getting past minding it.'

There was nothing more to be learned here, and, day breaking soon after, Sir Murray summoned two more of his men—a couple who had not been so harassed—and proceeded once more to drag the lake, more assistance and better implements being at the same time sent for.

But first he had himself rowed carefully

over the water, peering down as he went, but the dragging had fouled the lake, so that this was soon given up as useless, and Sir Murray was about once more to lower the grapnel, when one of the men pointed out, with scared face, what appeared to be the body of a man floating at a short distance.

To reach the spot took but a few moments, and one of the men reached over to draw in a coat and vest, saturated, so that it was a wonder they could have floated.

'His clothes, Sir Murray,' said the man, lifting up the coat, when, from the breast, a packet of letters fell out, the directions blurred with the action of the water; but on two of them plainly enough could still be read:

Captain Norton,
Merland Hall.

CHAPTER XXX.

'LET the lake be dragged until the body is found,' said Sir Murray Gernon, 'and set me ashore.'

The men obeyed, and watched their master with wondering eyes as he strode off towards the house, his brow knit, and head bent, for he wanted to be alone and to think.

Here was, he told himself, an awful confirmation of his suspicions; and now, rid of one enemy to his peace, he wanted to consider what should be his next step.

All that day he kept himself shut in his own room, merely giving a few instructions to his servants respecting the course to be taken with the prisoners, who were soon handed over into the custody of the police.

But, as might have been expected, Sir Murray Gernon could not fit together the pieces of the puzzle : he could not in his heart conclude that Norton had been associated with the burglarious party, and he was still brooding over the matter, when a note was placed in his hands—one which made him start as if stung by some venomous beast, and sit staring, with dilated eyes, till rage and disappointment got the better of surprise.

The note was very short, too, and merely to the effect that Captain Norton, while passing the park palings on the previous night, had heard an appeal for help, and had taken the liberty of trespassing that he might render some aid; but in the darkness and haste to get home and change his wet things, he had lost a portion of his clothes, containing letters of importance. Would Sir Murray Gernon kindly give orders that, if found, they might be restored?

Sir Murray Gernon sat for some minutes staring blankly at the paper as he mastered its contents. Here, then, was proof in the man's own handwriting that he had trespassed upon the Castle grounds on the previous night —but for what?

Reason gave the answer at once, but suspicion refused the explanation. There must have been some underhanded motive. Lady Gernon was dressed: she had not been to bed. Could it be that an evasion had been planned and interrupted by the fortuitous visit of the burglars? It must be so; and, feeling that he was now upon the right scent, Sir Murray determined to double his precautions, and acting on that determination, he stooped more and more to the meanness of acting the part of spy.

He would have challenged Norton to meet him again and again, but he told himself, with a grim smile, that he was a poltroon—as great a coward as ever breathed—and he felt more bitter than ever against him. It seemed to Sir Murray that he had been hoaxed—that he had been made the object of a trick that should for a few hours make him believe in Norton's death. He could not see that the acting of such a purposeless part would have been insensate to a degree, and that it was all due to the strength of his own imagination— an imagination now ever running riot in its wild theorizing.

Norton might have smiled could he have read Sir Murray's heart, in spite of the anger and pain he would have felt. For his own part, he had, on reaching the footway of the bridge, stood thoughtful for a few moments, and then, hearing Sir Murray's voice, had come to the conclusion that the better plan would be to hurry away, and so avoid an encounter, feeling sure that his acts would be, in some way or other, misconstrued. He trusted that it would be supposed he had made his way to a place of safety ; but, at all events, he was determined not to meet the baronet, and therefore pro-ceeded quickly homewards, little thinking of the conclusions that would be arrived at, till towards the evening of the day following, when he recalled the fact that his recognition was certain in consequence of the clothes he had lost, the result being that he sent the note above alluded to. The writing of this note involved a full account to Mrs Norton of the night's adventure, to her great discomfort, for beyond a bare outline given in explanation of the wet clothes, Mrs Norton had known little of the state of affairs. By degrees, though, that day the news of the attempted burglary had reached the Hall, and Norton comprehended the cause of the cry for help to which he had so opportunely responded. At the same time, though, he could not but regret that he had been the instrument called upon to save the men's lives, the uneasiness brought upon him by the incident being excessive—an uneasiness fully shared, though in silence, by his wife.

Events in the life of Mr John Gurdon about this time began to succeed each other with great rapidity. An examination before the county magistrates resulted in his committal, and the assizes coming on within a month, the ex-butler stood his trial. The evidence was too strong against him; he had been, as it were, taken red-handed, and, with his companions, was condemned to cross the seas to a land where there should be fewer temptations for him. The judge, taking all things into consideration, seemed to think that Gurdon's crime was more heinous even than that of his companions, and visited it accordingly; for, while the other two men were sentenced to transportation for fourteen years, John Gurdon's sentence was almost equivalent to condemnation for life, inasmuch as he was to be exiled for twenty years.

'All right, gentlemen—all right,' he said, coolly; 'but I shall come back again. And as for you, Sir Murray Gernon, I'll bear you in mind till my return; for I've not done with you and yours.'

'Remove him at once!' said the judge, and a couple of officers seized the prisoner, and hurried him from the dock.

'And now, don't be too hard on me, lassie,' said M'Cray, the day after the trial— for he had managed to encounter Jane in one of the passages—' don't be hard upon me, lassie, for I only did my duty.'

· 'I know—I know,' said Jane, sadly ; 'but please don't talk to me now.'

'Weel, weel, I know that your puir heart's sair yet, lassie, and I won't talk aboot sic things ; but talk to ye I must, aboot something.'

'You're as bad as a woman, Mr M'Cray,' said Jane, pettishly.

'I only wish I was half as good as one woman I ken,' said Sandy, gallantly. 'But hoot, lassie, I'm glad to see the Squire's coming round. He brought her leddyship with him into the garden yestreen, and told her he'd make me the head gairdener, and the puir thing leuked as bright and happy as could be ; and, d'ye ken, lassie, I think we're going to hae bright times again at the Castle, and I'm aboot setting things reet, and I'll be as busy as busy, day after day ; but ye'll see me a bit o' nichts ? '

' Did Sir Murray speak kindly to her ladyship ? ' said Jane anxiously.

' Kind ! ay,' said Sandy ; ' and she turned to him directly, and laid her hand upon his arm, and they strolled off together behind the bushes, and he passed his arm round her—so, Jenny—and stooped him down, and kissed her—just as I'm showing of ye—there, just on her bonnie cheek, like that ; for they didna ken I could see.'

As Sandy M'Cray gave his description with illustrations, Jane started angrily away.

' Nay, lassie, gude save us, she didna do so, for she turned her bonnie face up to his, and looked sae loving and airnest in his e'e, that it was quite a sight. And, Jenny, lassie, ain't ye glad I'm head-gairdener noo. I dinna care myself, but I thought ye'd be glad.'

'M'Cray,' exclaimed Jane, earnestly, as she came once more closer to him, 'you're a good and true-hearted man, and I'm not worthy of you.'

'Hoot—hoot! lassie; haud that clap.'

'But,' continued Jane, 'I've no one else to talk to and confide in. You are thoughtful and wise, and see a great deal, and then say nothing about it. You know how Sir Murray and my lady have been of late, and how he has behaved.'

'Yes—yes,' said Sandy; 'he's been feeling just as I used to feel when—'

'Don't, please—don't say any more about that.'

'Not I, lassie,' said Sandy, caressingly.

'But this soft way of his, now, I don't

like it,' said Jane. 'My life on it, he's never had any cause for his jealousy. I believe now it was all due to that wicked wretch saying things of my dear lady, and Sir Murray getting to hear of them.'

'Hoot, not so fast, lassie. What wicked wretch?'

'Oh, don't ask me,' said Jane, with pained face. 'You know who I mean.'

'So I do, lassie—so I do,' said Sandy, smiling, and softly rubbing his hands. 'But he'll do nae mair mischief.'

'Well,' said Jane, eagerly, 'I saw Sir Murray only this morning talking gently to my lady, and as soon as he left her, he was looking that evil, and muttering so, that it was horrible. I don't believe in him, and there's something wrong. She has offended him, and he hasn't forgiven her. You know how I love my lady.'

'Gude sake, yes, lassie, and I love ye for't.'

'And that dear, sweet babe! I don't think she loves it better herself. And only a night or two since she was down on her knees, crying fit to break her heart, by its side; and she said to me, "Jane—Jane, when something happens to me, be a mother to it; never leave her side, come what may."'

'And ye promised her?' said Sandy, earnestly.

'Of course,' exclaimed Jane, as she wiped her eyes.

'Gude lass—gude lass; and it's not me that will ask ye to. Ye shall watch over the little thing, Jenny, and I'll help ye. But what's she mean aboot when something happens her?'

'Oh, it's her low way, and I think she's afraid of Sir Murray; and now all this change in him isn't natural. I tell you, Alexander—'

'Gude; I like that,' muttered the Scot, as, in her earnestness, Jane laid her hand upon his arm.

'I tell you, that if anything happens to my dear lady, I shall think it's his doing.'

'Hoot—tut—tut! lassie, ye're giving way to strange thoughts, such as oughtn't to be in a Christian woman's heart. And now, lassie, I winna bother ye, but ye'll always talk to me like this, and come to me for counsel. I'm nae Solomon, Jenny, but I'll always tell ye the most I know. And there, there, little one, ye'll be my ain wife some day, winna ye?'

There must have been something very satisfactory in Jane's reply, for, after a few moment's silence, Alexander M'Cray went softly away upon the points of his boots, making his way into the garden, where he was soon busy superintending the improvement of flower-beds, and making alterations in spots that had long been an eyesore to him, inasmuch as they had been favourite whims of the now pensioned off, prejudiced old man, who had hitherto ruled the grounds.

'Gude sake, she's a real woman,' muttered Sandy, as he raised his cap to Lady Gernon, who, basket in hand, passed him on her way to the gates. 'I like to see a woman with a lo'e for flowers, even if they be the wild wee bits o' things she picks. But here comes the laird.'

68

CHAPTER XXXI.

UNDER ORDERS.

SANDY M'CRAY, in spite of his dignity as
head 'gairdner,' was not above working
hard himself, and he was busy enough when,
slowly and gloomily, Sir Murray made his appearance, looking anxiously about the grounds,
as if in search of something he could not see.
He went first in one direction, then in another,
and at last he returned to where Sandy was
busy.

'Has her ladyship passed this way, gardener?' he said.

'Yes, Sir Mooray, a quarter of an hour syne. She took the path for the north gate.'

Sir Murray Gernon bent his head by way of thanks, and walked slowly down the path till he had passed round the house, when he started off walking swiftly, making for the north gate, through which he passed, and then walked hurriedly on.

There was the wife of one of the under-gardeners at the lodge ready to drop him a courtesy, and from her he could, no doubt, have learned in a moment which direction her ladyship had taken, but he refrained from asking; and, evidently with an idea that he knew the place to which she would resort, he took a narrow path leading off towards a wood, one of the few old forests yet left in England; but, after walking quite half an hour, always anxiously peering to right or left, he seemed to be at fault, and turned sharply back to go in another direction, this time almost at a run.

That he was much agitated was plain enough, for though his face, and even his lips, were white, the veins in his forehead stood out in a perfect network, his pulses, too, throbbing fiercely. Twice over a heavy bead of perspiration trickled down his face, but he heeded it not, but, evidently now settled upon the point he sought, he passed rapidly along a by-path which led into one of the inner recesses of the wood.

Sir Murray had not left the garden ten minutes when, rising from his work for an instant, M'Cray became aware of the flutter of a dress in the distance, and the next instant made out that the wearer was Jane Barker, who now signalled him to come to her.

' And me so busy, too,' muttered the gardener. ' I did say that all my bit of courting should be done of an evening ; and here's a temptation, coming in the middle of the day. But there, gude save us, I must go when she calls, if I lose my place.'

' And there ye are, then,' he said, as he reached the place where Jane was anxiously awaiting him, 'the brightest flower in the garden, lassie.'

' Oh, Alexander!' ejaculated Jane.

' Bless ye for that, my bairn! Ye've taken, then, to ca' me by my name at last.'

'Pray—pray make haste and help me. What shall I do?'

'Do, lassie,' exclaimed the downright Scot. ' Why, tell me what's the matter.'

' Yes, yes,' cried the agitated girl. ' You know my lady went out a little while since.'

' Ay, I saw her go.'

' And then Sir Murray came down.'

' To be sure, and he askit me the which way she'd gone.'

'Yes, yes,' cried Jane, 'and I went up on
to the top of the house on the leads, and I've
been watching him, and he's followed her.'

'To be sure, lassie; and wadna I ha'e
done the same if ye'd gone the same
gait?'

'Oh yes—no,—I don't know,' said Jane ;
'but I don't like it, and I want you to follow
them.'

'Me? Follow? What, go after Sir Mooray
and my lady?' exclaimed M'Cray. 'Hoot,
lassie, and have ye gone daft ?'

'Daft ! no !' cried Jane, angrily. 'You
must—indeed, you must go after them. He
came to me quite angry when he found that
her ladyship had gone out, and asked me
where I thought she'd be ; and I told him,
like the fool that I was ; and I don't like
things—I don't, indeed; and I'm afraid there's
mischief on the way.'

'My dear bairn,' said the thoughtful Scot, 'I'm afraid ye've been letting your fancy run away with ye full galop. Once you women get an idea into your poor little heads ye go racing after it full tear. Now, let me ask ye what is there strange in my lady going out to pick specimens, as she's done hundreds o' times before? and, now that they're making it up, for Sir Mooray to go after her?'

'Nothing—nothing,' said Jane, earnestly, 'if it were all genuine; but, Alexander—dear Alexander, there's Judas kisses as well as true ones, and I know he did not mean what you saw. I'm troubled about it all, and I come to you for help: don't fail me, please, now this first time.'

'Nay, nay,' cried the Scot, eagerly. 'I'll not fail thee, lassie. But what am I to do? Where am I to go?'

'Follow them and watch them, never leaving them for an instant, and always being ready to give help.'

' Yes, yes ; I'll do it, lassie.'

' I knew you would,' cried Jane, pressing his great hand between both of hers ; 'and now run—run all the way, for he went to his room after he left me, and came out pushing a pistol into his pocket. And, oh ! Alexander, if you love me, make haste, for I'm sure that there's something wrong ! '

CHAPTER XXXII.

WHAT SANDY DID NOT SEE.

'GUDE save us!' muttered M'Cray, as he set off round the house at a sharp trot —' Gude save us and ha'e maircy! Here's a pretty pickle for an upper gairdner. Only just got my promotion, and I shall be brought down again as sure as my name's Sandy M'Cray. Trust the lassies for getting ye into a mess. Only foregather with one of the pretty things, and ye'll be in a mess before long. Gude save us! what shall I do? He'll be savage with me as a dog-otter. Nay, I ken what I'll do.'

A bright thought had evidently crossed Sandy's mind, for, turning suddenly, he dodged into the kitchen-garden, and round by the tool-house, heralding his coming, a minute after, by a loud rattle, as he appeared, trundling a wheel-barrow, in which he had hastily thrown a basket and a three-pronged fork.

'I'm after ferns for the new rockery, to be sure!' he said, with a grin; and then away he spun at a tremendous rate, dashing along to the north gate, and bringing the woman out to see whether he had gone mad.

'Don't go that way, Mr M'Cray!' cried the woman after him, as she saw him turn down the path which led to the wood. 'Sir Murray and my lady have gone that way.'

'Gude save us, that's the right news!' muttered Sandy; and the barrow rattled more loudly than ever, as he dashed along till he came to an alley, down which, a good quarter of a mile from where he stood, he could see Sir Murray and Lady Gernon.

'There they are, then,' he muttered; and running the barrow aside, he took out basket and fork, and began to thread his way amongst the trees, so as to approach unseen close to where his master and Lady Gernon were walking.

But Sandy M'Cray was a cautious man, and before he had gone many yards he had stooped to dig up half-a-dozen hart's-tongue ferns, which he placed, with a fair quantity of leaf-mould, in his basket.

'There's my answer to whatever they speer,' he muttered; and then, creeping cautiously forward, he made his way to where, by holding aside the hazel boughs, he could peer out into the alley, where in a few minutes he saw the couple he watched pass by within a couple of yards of where he stood, silently and without hardly a rustle of the leaves amongst which they passed.

But just as they had gone by they stopped short, Lady Gernon holding tightly by Sir Murray's arm, as she gazed, with a wild, eager stare in his face.

'We had better make haste back, Lady Gernon,' he said, quietly, and with a peculiar smile; and then they walked on.

'There, now! What could be better than that?' said M'Cray, as soon as he was alone. 'She looks pale, but they were quiet enow. But what did he mean by showing his teeth to her when he smilt?'

Sandy M'Cray shook his head, and then, in obedience to his instructions, he followed slowly, contriving from time to time to keep the couple in sight, but ever and anon shaking his head as if something troubled him. At last he said, half aloud:

'The lassie is richt, after a'. There's your gude, sweet kiss, and your Judas kiss, and I think perhaps she did richt in sending me; but it's a sair job to leave one's work i' the daytime, and after a' there was not much to come for.'

Had Sandy M'Cray been there five—nay, four—minutes sooner, he would have been of a different opinion, for Sir Murray Gernon, led, perhaps, by some tricksy sprite of the woods—some Puck of modern times—had hurried on and on, each moment growing more and more angry and excited at having missed the object of his search. For days past she had never left the Castle unwatched, but this time she had gone out suddenly, and at an hour when he had believed her to be in her bedroom. That there was some definite object for her walk he felt convinced, and when, after hurrying up and down several alleys of the wood, he at length caught sight of Lady Gernon, he felt no surprise—there was no great feeling of mad anger in his breast, but something like a bitter sense of satisfaction, such as might be that of any one who, after a long and arduous search, comes upon the object of his quest.

He uttered no exclamation, made no excited movement; but, with such a smile as M'Cray had described, he stood gazing down a woodland arcade, to where, some fifty yards in advance—framed, as it were, in the autumn-tinted leaves—stood Lady Gernon and the man to whom she had first given her love.

They were, perhaps, a yard apart—Lady Gernon, with her head bent, resting with one hand against a tree-trunk; Philip Norton—his hands upon the stick he held—gazing at her, it seemed, sadly and earnestly; but, as far as Sir Murray could tell, no word was spoken.

The next moment, quietly, and still smiling, Sir Murray slowly advanced down the arcade, half of which he had traversed before he was perceived; but even then there was no start—no guilty confusion—only Lady Gernon turned deadly pale, and a shade of trouble crossed Captain Norton's face.

Sir Murray, with the same strange smile, advanced to where they stood, raising his hat in answer to Norton's salute; and then, with the most courteous air, he said:

'Lady Gernon, you look pale.'

'I believe, Sir Murray,' said Norton, 'Lady Gernon was startled and troubled at our sudden encounter.'

'Exactly,' said Sir Murray, quietly.

'You misunderstand me,' said Norton, gravely, the shadow deepening upon his face. 'I alluded to her encounter with me. Five minutes since, I met her by accident.'

'Most accurate,' said Sir Murray, smiling.

'And after the past—after the misunder-
standing between our families, Sir Murray,'
continued Norton, not heeding the taunt—

'Exactly ?' said Sir Murray.

'I was sorry that the meeting should have
taken place. Lady Gernon,' he said, turning to
her, as he raised his hat, 'I will deliver your
message. It is, I know, both pain and sorrow
to dear Ada that you should be apart. Still,
I think it is for the best. Rest assured, though,
that the love you sent her is yours in return.
Heaven bless you! Good-bye, Sir Murray
Gernon!' he said, turning to the smiling
baronet—who stood with one hand buried in
his breast-pocket—'I am sorry for the past ;
but it is irrevocable, and I still repeat that I
am sorry for this encounter. Lady Gernon
seems pale and ill. Good day.'

He held out his hand quietly and frankly to

the baronet, though he had forborne to do so to his lady, and there was an air of calm innocence in his aspect, that should have carried with it conviction; but Sir Murray never stirred; his hand was still buried in his breast, as, with a mocking smile, he said :

'Captain Norton, the army was never your vocation, any more than the losing office of mine-director.'

'I do not understand you, Sir Murray,' was the calm, sad reply, as for a moment Norton's eyes met Marion Gernon's imploring glance.

'Indeed,' said the baronet, who had not lost the speaking look interchanged. 'I meant that fortune awaited you upon the stage ; you should have been an actor.'

The colour seemed to fade from Norton's face at these galling words, and the great blue scar stood out more prominently than ever;

but the next moment turning his gaze from Sir
Murray, he fixed his eyes upon Marion with a
soft, earnest, speaking look, that meant
volumes; for, changing in an instant from a
mocking smile to a look of rage and hate,
Sir Murray Gernon drew a pistol from his
pocket, and at a couple of paces' distance
presented it full at Norton. His finger
was upon the trigger—the weapon was fully
cocked—and even the slightest contraction of
the angry man's muscles would have sent the
contents through Philip Norton's breast. But
he did not wince—not a muscle moved; the
man who had before now stood deadly fire,
stood firm, till, with an oath, Sir Murray
hurled the pistol into the thicket, and led his
wife away.

But before they had gone a dozen yards
the smile had come back upon his lip, and he

turned to gaze at Lady Gernon, to see on her countenance the same old stony, despairing look that had been there on the wedding morn.

CHAPTER XXXIII.

JANE'S SUSPICIONS.

IT is quite possible that in his heart of hearts Sir Murray Gernon had doubts as to who had been the spoiler of his family jewels, but he would admit nothing to his breast but such thoughts as were disparaging to Norton.

At the Castle nods and smiles were prevalent, and the servants gossiped respecting the happy change that had taken place, arguing all sorts of gaieties once more ; for—so they said—the old house had been like a dungeon lately, and almost unbearable.

But there were doubts still in the minds of both Jane Barker and her lover, the former watching Sir Murray as narrowly as ever he watched his lady. There was a feeling of uneasiness in Jane's heart that grew stronger every day, a feeling not based upon any confidences of Lady Gernon's—for, though invariably kind and gentle, Marion was not cne to make a friend and counsellor of her servant —but upon Jane's own observation. The scraps she gathered she pieced together, and, when alone, tried to form some definite course of action—a trial resulting in a rigid determination which she followed out.

What took place in private was never known, but the pallor upon Lady Gernon's cheeks grew daily of a more sickly hue. A physician was sent for from the county town with great ostentation by Sir Murray, and shortly after, another from London, resulting

in prescriptions and medicine, which her ladyship took daily, such medicine being always
administered by Jane, who made a point, for
some reason or another, of leaving the bottles
always upon the table in her ladyship's dressing-room; and this went on for quite a couple
of months, the sickness increasing, though not
sufficiently to confine Lady Gernon to her
room. The walks, though, were pretty well
given up, and it was only at very rare intervals
that Lady Gernon strayed beyond the bound-
aries of the park.

The servants said that no one could be
more attentive than Sir Murray now was, and
that it was quite pleasant to see the alteration.
But Jane said nothing, she merely tightened
her lips, making no confidant; for once—
twice, four different times—she had encountered Sir Murray coming from her mistress's
dressing-room; and once, after such a visit,

when she went to give Lady Gernon her daily medicine, the poor girl fainted away upon learning that her duty had been forestalled by Sir Murray himself.

Whatever might have been Jane Barker's suspicions, she felt that this could not go on for ever; and worn out, and sick at heart, she one day put on her bonnet, ordered M'Cray to act as her escort, and made her way to Merland Hall.

Mrs Norton welcomed her heartily, but almost in dread, not knowing what interpretation might be placed upon the visit, should it come to Sir Murray's ears. But, to her great astonishment, Jane's first act was to close the window, and then, crossing the room, she turned the key in the lock; when, coming back close to the astonished occupant of the room, she threw herself down upon her knees, sobbing wildly; and catching hold of Ada's hand, she kissed it fiercely again and again.

'Is anything wrong?' exclaimed Ada Norton, with a horrified look, for a dreadful fear had flashed across her mind.

'No, Miss Ada—I mean Mrs Norton—*not yet—not yet!* but unless some one interferes there soon will be! Oh, 'm! I didn't care to go to the Rectory, for I knew that they wouldn't believe me there! but I'm afraid something dreadful will happen to my poor dear lady! I have come to you because you are her cousin, and I know you loved her, though things have gone so crooked since. But what shall we do, 'm? for since that last time when my lady met Mr Norton in the wood, and Sir Murray caught them—'

Jane ceased, for Ada Norton leaped to her feet as if some galvanic shock had passed through her frame.

'Oh, what am I saying, ma'am? I

didn't think that you'd take it in that way,
nor yet that you wouldn't know of it. It was
nothing, ma'am; only Sir Murray was telling
my lady of it; and she said that they met
by accident, and that almost all her words to
him were to send her love to you, ma'am.'

'It was, then, upon that occasion?' said
Ada Norton, in agitated tones.

'Yes, 'm; and I was in the dressing-
room, and heard all. Not that Sir Murray
spoke angrily, but in a curious, sneering tone
that frightens my lady; and ever since then
she's been ill, and taking medicine; and—oh,
'm!—you would not get me into trouble for
trying to do what's right by my lady?'

'No—no,' said Ada, who was trying to
recall her husband's words when he had told
her of his last meeting with Lady Gernon, for
he had said nothing respecting the coming of
Sir Murray.

'Well, ma'am,' sobbed Jane, 'since then'
—she sank her voice into a whisper, and sent
a thrill of horror through Ada Norton as she
spoke—' since then, ma'am, I'm sure Sir
Murray has been trying to poison her!'

'Poison my cousin, Lady Gernon?' exclaimed Ada. 'Nonsense! Absurd! Jane,
you are mad!'

'I hope I am, ma'am, about that—indeed
I do!' cried Jane, earnestly.

'But what have you seen? What do you
know?' exclaimed Mrs Norton.

'I haven't seen anything, ma'am, except
Sir Murray coming sometimes out of the
dressing-room, where the medicine's kept;
and I don't know anything except that my
lady's medicine always tastes different, and
looks different, when it's been in the dressing-
room a day or two; and every week it turns
a darker colour, and tastes stronger than it

did the week before. And besides all that, though Sir Murray smiles, and pretends to talk pleasant to the poor dear, suffering angel, than whom a better woman never lived, he hates her dreadfully, and more and more every day.'

'And how long has this been going on?' said Mrs Norton, with a faint smile.

'Weeks now, ma'am,' said Jane. 'But I see you don't believe me.'

'I believe you to be a good, affectionate girl, Jane,' said Mrs Norton, 'and that you love your mistress; but this seems to me to be a fearful and perfectly unfounded suspicion —one that I am glad, for every one's sake, that you have hinted to no one else. Think of the absurdity of the thing. This has, you say, been going on for weeks; and yet, you see, your mistress is not poisoned yet.'

'No, ma'am, not yet,' said Jane, meaningly.

'Well, then, my good girl, how do you account for that?'

'Because, ma'am,' said Jane, in a whisper, 'she's never taken any of the medicine but once.'

'How? What do you mean?' exclaimed Mrs Norton.

'I've managed to get the stuff made up at two places, ma'am,' whispered Jane. 'One lot's fetched by the footman from one chemist's, at Marshton, and I get the gardener to go to another chemist's for the other. I only had to send the doctor's paper, and the medicine comes just like what Sir Murray knows is sent for.'

'Well,' exclaimed Ada, impatiently.

'Well, 'm,' whispered Jane, 'that which her ladyship takes I keep locked up, and that which stands on the dressing-table gets poured out of the window, a little at a time, upon the flower-beds.'

Ada Norton sat silently gazing at Jane for a few minutes before she spoke.

'Jane,' she said, 'this is a fearful charge!' and she shuddered. 'I must think about it, and before many hours I will come over to the Castle, and see either Sir Murray or Lady Gernon. Do not be afraid; I will not implicate you in any way. I must see Mr Elstree, and I will try to make some plan—to arrange something definite; but your words have confused me—-almost taken away my breath. The thing seems so monstrous, and even now I cannot believe it true! But I should not feel that I had done my duty if, after what you have said, I did not take some steps; so rest assured that I will do something, and at once.'

Jane rose to go, and, trembling and excited, Ada Norton sat for some hours, pondering whether she should ask her husband's advice, ending by putting it off till the next day, when it happened that it was out of her power.

CHAPTER XXXIV.

NOT AT HOME.

'DID you see the laird?' said M'Cray, coming slowly forth from behind some bushes, after Jane had been standing some few minutes in the lane where she had left him to wait.

'The laird!' said Jane, starting. 'Why, who do you mean?'

'Mean? Why, Sir Mooray himself. I saw him turn round to have a good look at ye, as ye came across the home close from the Hall. And ye didna see him?'

'No—no—no!' sobbed Jane. 'Oh dear
—oh dear! I'm undone!'

'Nay—nay, ye're not, lassie; for I'll
a'ways stand by ye. Dinna greet aboot that.
Ye didna tell me why ye came, but I know it's
for some good, and that ye'll tell me all in
good time.'

'That I will, indeed!' sobbed Jane; 'but
don't ask me now!'

'Nay, then, I'm not speering to know,'
said Sandy, contentedly. 'He was riding the
gray horse, ye ken, and he seemed to catch
sight o' ye all at aince; when, thinking it
wasna warth while for twa to be in trouble, I
hid myself in the bushes till he'd gone by.'

The next day, one anxiously looked forward to by more than one of the characters in
this story, came in due course; and, towards
evening, Lady Gernon slowly passed through
the hall door, basket in hand, and making her

way across the lawn, disappeared from the sight of Sandy M'Cray behind some bushes at the edge of the park.

The hours sped on, and Ada Norton drove up in one of Chunt's flys from the village public-house, after waiting some time at the Rectory, in a vain endeavour to see Mr Elstree, who was from home. She had, after many hours' thought, but a vague idea of the best plan to pursue, and even now questioned the wisdom of her course. In fact, more than once the check-string had been in her hand to arrest the driver, and order him to return to the Hall; but, from sheer shame at her vacillation, she let it fall again, and gazed slowly out from the fly-window at the glorious sweep of the noble domain through which she was being driven, and sighed again and again as she thought of the misery of its owners. She half shrank from meeting Lady Gernon, for she felt that, in spite of all her assurances to the contrary, her cousin must feel something of repugnance to the woman who had, as it were, taken her place. Not that she had robbed Lady Gernon of her happiness; she had been ready to resign all hope, and had given up, stifling her own feelings, when duty told her that she was called upon so to act. But could Marion feel the same?

She asked herself that question as the fly drove up to the noble front of the great mansion; and then, rousing herself for the task in hand, she prepared to meet her cousin.

'Not at home,' was the answer given by the footman to the driver; when Ada beckoned the man to the fly door—a slow-speaking, insolent menial, who had, before now, performed Sir Murray's best in acting the part of spy.

'I think,' said Ada, 'that my cousin would

see me, even if she is confined to her room.'

'Sir Murray give orders, mum, that they were not at home to visitors from the Hall; and, besides, my lady ain't in.'

Ada Norton felt that it was cowardly, but it was with a sense of relief that she sank back against the cushions, and began to turn over in her mind what course she ought to pursue. She dreaded the exciting effect it might have upon her husband, if she revealed to him the words she had heard from Jane; and, trembling with an anxiety she could not drive away, she returned to the Hall, to find that Captain Norton had gone out.

'Packed a carpet bag, ma'am,' said the servant, 'and then wrote a note for you, after sending for Master Brace, and kissing him.'

The note was on the table, and snatching it up, Ada Norton read as follows :—

'Dearest Ada,—

'Do not think hardly of me. I could not help myself; but I know you will not judge me harshly. More when I write again; but *give no information of my movements to a soul.* I shall be away some time, but I have made full arrangements with Garland & Son about you.   Philip.'

Abrupt, enigmatical, and strange; but it was like him. There was a vein of affection, though, running through it all. He had made arrangements for her; but the tears dimmed Ada Norton's eyes as she stood with the letter in her hands. What could it all mean? she thought. Had it anything to do with the mining transaction? Should she drive over to Marshton the next day, and ask Messrs Garland & Son, her husband's solicitors? No, she would not do that; it would be like prying into his affairs. She had always had faith in him, so far, and that faith should continue to the end.

She dashed away the tears heroically, little thinking how soon and how sorely she was to be tried. It was nothing new for Norton to absent himself, and she could wait patiently for his return, 'Like a good wife,' she said, smilingly; and then, sitting down, she took her work, but only for it to fall into her lap, as she tried to divine what would be her best plan to adopt in connection with the strange information which had the day before been imparted to her.

CHAPTER XXXV.

A STORM AT MERLAND.

SIR MURRAY GERNON had, during the
past few weeks, made a good deal of use
of his horses—another sign, the stablemen ob-
served, of a returning good state of things, for
they were growing quite tired of doing nothing
but taking the horses out for exercise.   But Sir
Murray's rides were only round and about his
own estate : he never went far, though he was
out for hours at a time ; and the day before
there was again a fierce look upon his face, as

he caught sight of Jane Barker hurriedly leaving Merland Hall.

'Of course!' he said; he might have known that before. Time proved all things, and here, at length, was before his eyes the arrangement by which letters and messages had been conveyed.

But he was, if anything, more than usually courteous to my lady that evening at dinner. Sir Murray hadn't been in such a good temper for long enough past, said one of the footmen; only my lady looked so ill and sad, and shivered so. It was almost a pity she should have come down to dinner.

Sir Murray had been out again, riding up and down forest paths, and by copse edges, along by field and meadow; and always with his head bent, and a watchful look in his eye.

About an hour after Ada Norton's visit to the Castle, Sir Murray slowly walked his horse up to the door, and the footman ran down the steps, and laid his hand on the animal's neck.

'Stand aside a few minutes, William,' said Sir Murray; and the groom, who had also run up to take the saddle-horse, touched his hat and fell back. 'Well, what now?' he exclaimed hastily, for something in the footman's face told of tidings.

'I thought I'd better tell you, Sir Murray,' said the man, 'her ladyship—'

'Not—?' ejaculated Sir Murray, starting, and turning livid, as he checked himself. 'Has the doctor been sent for?'

'No, Sir Murray,' said the man; 'her ladyship ain't worse, only she went out this afternoon.'

'Well?' said the baronet.

'That's all, Sir Murray,' said the man, timidly. 'I was called away, and didn't see her go. I didn't know it till just now, when one of the gardeners said he saw her go out, and he thought the pony-carriage ought to be sent for her, as a storm was coming on.'

'She has not come back, then?' exclaimed Sir Murray; and then, clapping spurs to his horse, he made it dash forward; but only to check it the next instant, rein back, and descend, beckoning up the groom, and then slowly mounting the steps.

' You have not said a word of all this?' said the baronet, in a low tone.

' Not a word, Sir Murray !' exclaimed the man, with an injured air. ' You can trust me, sir.'

Sir Murray Gernon smiled bitterly, as he threw his hat and gloves to the man, and entered his library, leaving the door open, and watching for Lady Gernon's return.

An hour elapsed, and then he rang.

'No, Sir Murray; her ladyship has not returned.'

Another hour passed, and the storm prophesied of by Alexander M'Cray was at hand. First came a deep gloom; then the sighing of the wind in faint puffs, as it swept round the house; then there was a flash or two of lightning, and the muttering of thunder; then flash after flash lighting up the heavens, succeeded by a darkness as of the blackest night. A few minutes seemed to elapse, as if Nature was preparing herself for a grand effort; and then, with a mighty, rushing crash, down came the main body of the storm, of which the previous mutterings had been but the *avant-garde*. The rain seemed to fall in one vast sheet, through which the blue lightning cut and flickered; while, with a deafening roar, peal after peal of thunder seemed to burst over the mansion, threatening it with destruction.

'Should the pony-carriage be brought round, sir?' asked the footman, shouting to make himself heard.

'Yes,' said Sir Murray, 'and my horse. Send M'Cray, the gardener, here, too.'

M'Cray, who had been trying to console Jane, who was greatly agitated, soon made his appearance before Sir Murray.

'M'Cray, take one of the horses, and go round from cottage to cottage till you find where her ladyship has taken refuge. Williams, you go south with the pony-carriage, and I shall ride east.'

The gardener saluted, and ten minutes after, heedless of the storm—though he had hard work with his frightened beast—he was mounted, amidst the sneers of the grooms, who looked upon such missions as within their province, and resented the coming of the interloper accordingly.

'The puir weak body! But I'll soon find her,' muttered M'Cray, as he cantered on out at the park gates; and then going from cottage to cottage, and at last entering the forest, and riding between the dripping trees, and along the slippery clay paths to the different keepers' houses, but without avail; so that, at last, thoroughly soaked and disheartened, he turned back, feeling sure that, before that time, her ladyship must have returned.

'Not come back,' whispered one of the grooms to him, as he entered the yard. 'Williams got back an hour agone, and Sir Murray has been in and gone out again.'

Just at that moment, with his horse in a foam, Sir Murray galloped up.

'Well?' he said, eagerly.

'No one has even seen her leddyship, Sir Mooray,' said the gardener, curtly.

'The same answer everywhere!' exclaimed the baronet. ' Let every man mount and set off. Tell the keepers to search the wood. You, M'Cray, come with me, unless Williams has returned.'

' Williams is so wet, sir, he's gone to bed,' said a man.

' Quick, then, M'Cray ! ' exclaimed Sir Murray; ' and keep that tongue of yours silent afterwards ! '

' Ye may trust me, Sir Mooray,' said M'Cray, gruffly; and setting off at a smart canter, they were soon nearing the village street.

The storm had by this time passed over, and the stars were blinking out here and there; but from every tree and leaf the great drops fell pattering down, while ditch and channel ran furiously with their unwonted muddy currents.

' Go into that public-house, and ask what

conveyances have gone out from there to-day —this afternoon?' said Sir Murray.

M'Cray returned in five minutes, followed by the inquisitive Chunt.

'Good evening, Sir Murray,' he said, hat in hand, and not seeing the frown upon the baronet's countenance. 'I've been telling your man, Sir Murray, nothing's gone but the dog-cart as Cap'en Norton came and had out. Carried his bag over, sir, and wouldn't wait for a man to bring the car back; said he'd drive himself, and leave it at 'The Chequers,' at Marshton, Sir Murray.'

The mud from the horse's hoofs was splashed in Chunt's face as he finished, for Sir Murray stuck in the spurs so, that the poor brute plunged furiously; and it was all that M'Cray—not the best of horsemen—could do to overtake him, as he galloped along the main road to Marshton, where they arrived about ten, with their horses blown, and covered with foam, Sir Murray, who had not spoken, leading the way into the inn-yard.

'Chunt's dog-car, sir? Brought in here about five, sir, by a boy as a gent gave six-pence to bring it in, sir. Tall gent, with a mark across his face, sir,' the boy said.

So spake 'The Chequers'' hostler, in reply to questions put by Sir Murray Gernon, who had drawn his hat down over his eyes, and turned up the collar of his coat, as though to prevent his being recognized.

'What boy, sir? Can't say, sir. Looked like lad returning from harvest work. Quite a stranger to these parts, sir.'

Without another word, Sir Murray Gernon turned his horse's head, and rode out of the yard, followed by M'Cray, who clung to him as if he had been his shadow; but the horses were now tired, unused as they were to much exertion, and it was getting close upon midnight when the baronet and his servant rode into the stable-yard at Merland Castle.

Sir Murray asked no questions. It was plain enough, from the silence, that there was no news; so throwing his bridle to a groom, his act was closely imitated by M'Cray, who followed him into the library.

'I'm sorry for the puir body, wherever she is,' muttered M'Cray; 'but, perhaps, after all, there's naething the matter. Onyhow, such a ride, and such a wetting, desarves a drappie of toddy, and perhaps Sir Mooray may ask me to take it. I'll follow him, anyhow, for how do I know whether he's done wi' me?'

CHAPTER XXXVI.

JANE DECLARES.

M'CRAY stood watching his master with attentive eye, as, apparently ignorant of his presence, the baronet—drenched as he was with rain and perspiration—threw himself into a chair, and covered his face with his hands.

The gardener stood on one leg, then on the other, then leaned on a chair-back, putting himself into every posture that would give him a little ease, for he was well-nigh exhausted. But no notice took Sir Murray. He was apparently buried in himself; and, at last, unable to draw his attention by coughing and shuffling about, Sandy M'Cray prepared to speak.

'He's greeting aboot her, puir laddie,' he muttered to himself; 'but, a' the same, he might ha' brought out the whuskee. We're mair free with the wee drappie up north.' Then, aloud: 'Hoot, then, Sir Mooray, it's a bad habit to sit in wet clouts. Hadna ye better tak' just a wet o' some kind o' sperrits? I think a little whuskee wad do ye nae hairm.'

'You here still?' exclaimed Sir Murray; and then, angrily, as a hand was laid upon the handle of the door: 'Who's that? I am engaged.'

But the door opened, and, to Sandy M'Cray's astonishment, Jane crept in, white as a sheet, as if from some great horror; but, all the same, carrying tenderly, as she hushed it to sleep, the little child that, after five years, had been born to Sir Murray.'

'Hoot, lassie! and what do ye do here?'

'What do I do?' exclaimed Jane, fiercely, her half-frightened aspect giving place to a look of rage. 'I have come to ask that man what he has done with my dear lady!'

'Hoot, lassie! do ye ken it's the laird?' exclaimed the alarmed gardener; and then, stooping over her, he put his face close to hers, and muttered to himself: 'There isna a smell of the stuff on her mooth, or I'd say she'd been at the whuskee.'

'Stand aside, M'Cray!' she said hoarsely. 'I want to ask him, I tell you, what he has done with my dear lady.'

After the manner of a woman of her class, she raised her voice as she spoke; when, in alarm, the Scot darted to and closed the door, turning the little inside bolt, and then hurrying back to his betrothed's side; for there was something threatening in the baronet's looks, as he rose from his chair, glaring the while at his wife's maid.

'Stand back, M'Cray!' cried Jane, hoarsely, as he laid his hand upon her arm. 'I've been silent all these months, but I'll speak now. Let him strike me if he dares, but he dare not! See here!' she cried, 'I've brought your little one down to you, to see if it will do anything towards melting your hard, proud, cruel heart, and making you tell the truth! Tell me now, and at once, what you have done with my dear lady!'

'Take her away, and this instant!' hissed Sir Murray. 'The woman's mad!'

'Mad! No, I am not mad! Keep back, M'Cray; I won't go! Touch me again, and I'll scream so as to alarm the house; and then all the servants shall hear what I mean to say

to you alone. I'm not afraid, I tell you, and
I will be answered. But, oh, Sir Murray!'
she cried, softening for a moment, 'tell me
where the poor thing is! What have you
done with her?'

'You Scotch wolf!' exclaimed Sir Murray,
in a rage, to the gardener, 'why do you not
take the mad fool from my sight?'

M'Cray placed his arm round Jane, and
tried to lead her off; but she struggled from
him, and uttered a wild, piercing scream that
made him start aside, as if the shrill sound
had pierced him like a sword.

'I will not go!' cried the girl, stamping
with fury. 'I will know first! Do you
think I am to be cheated and blinded by all
this pretended hunting to find my poor
darling, ill-used lady? Why did you come,
with your pride and your money, to her happy
home, and take her away to be your miserable

wife? Why did you ever come near the poor, sweet innocent? And then, after all her suffering, to insult her with your cruel, base suspicions, so unmanly—so false!'

'Curse the woman! Am I to strike her in the mouth?' raged Sir Murray, in a hoarse whisper; for there were voices to be heard outside — evidently those of the servants, alarmed by the wild shriek, and once the door was softly tried.

'Na—na, Sir Mooray!' said M'Cray; 'nae blows to a woman. The puir thing's daft wi' grief and passion, and greeting after her lady; but she'll be better therectly. Whush, then, Jenny, let's gang our gait, and leave the laird to himsel'.'

'If you touch me again, M'Cray, I'll alarm the house!' cried Jane; and the great Scot fell back once more, as going closer to Sir Murray Gernon, she continued, hoarsely:

'You've been making your plans for long enough, and this is a part of them! It will blind some people, but it won't me. I've been watching, as well as you; for my heart bled to see the poor, ill-used, neglected, tortured thing pining away, day after day! But Heaven will judge you for this, and bring down punishment upon you! She knew it was coming: she shuddered, and talked of dying, and begged of me to be a mother to her poor little one, and I swore I would; and I will, poor humble servant as I am! But right makes me strong, while wrong makes you weak and a coward, so that you are afraid, and obliged to listen to me. I'm not afraid of your fierce looks, for it shall all out, if I go to the magistrates myself. Hunting round, looking for her, you false, cruel traitor! Do you think you could deceive me? You listened for some purpose to the cruel lies of that wretch

Gurdon, who ought to have had his tongue cut out; and now that you have planned and plotted, you think we are all cheated, but you are wrong. I don't care who hears me, I will speak, and I say it now. Look at him, M'Cray: you are a bold, honest man, before whom he cowers—this great baronet, with his title—like a beaten hound! I tell you that for weeks past he has been trying to poison— '

With an exclamation of rage Sir Murray rushed at her; but she never flinched.

'To poison my dear lady!' exclaimed Jane.

'Hush—hush! for Heaven's sake, hush, woman!' cried Sir Murray; and in an instant he had placed his hand over her mouth.

But it was only for an instant; M'Cray

had dragged him from her, as, reeling as she spoke, Jane gasped:

'Keep him from me; his hands are yet red! I tell you, as I will tell the world, if I live, my lady is not lost, but murdered!'

CHAPTER XXXVII.

SIR MURRAY DECLARES.

'SEND those people away from the door!
Make her be silent; the woman's mad!'
exclaimed Sir Murray excitedly, as, shrinking
back, he stood, trembling and haggard, before
M'Cray. 'It's all nonsense—folly—that she
has said. No; keep her here till those people
have gone.'

'Ye'll be quiet noo, lassie, winna ye?'
said M'Cray soothingly, as he held Jane in
his arms, and then placed her in a chair,
when the mad excitement that had kept her

SIR MURRAY DECLARES. 125

up so far seemed to desert her; and bowing down over the frightened child, she kissed and hushed it to sleep, sobbing over it hysterically, and every now and then breaking into a wail of misery. She took no further notice of her master, who gazed at her with an aspect of alarm, fearing, apparently, to speak, lest he might bring forth another such outbreak as the last. But he had no cause for fear; Jane was now tractable as a child, as M'Cray soon found; and going close to Sir Murray, he whispered:

'That's an ower thick door, Sir Mooray, as I fun oot when I brak' it open. They didna hear what was said by the puir thing, half daft with grief; and gin ye'll trust me, I'll see that she doesna talk ony more sic stuff.'

Sir Murray did not answer,—he merely bowed his head; for there was a battle going on in his breast—a strife between dread and mortification at having to humble himself before his own servants. It was hard work to arrest the groan that struggled for exit, and when the door closed on Sandy M'Cray and Jane, he sank back in his chair as if stunned.

M'Cray felt that Sir Murray's silence gave consent, and that he was trusted. The trust, too, was not misplaced; for the Scot had obtained sufficient influence over Jane to reason her, in her calmer moments, into silence.

'Supposing, even, that you're right, lassie, ye ken that the puir bodie we've lost wadna have wished ye to bring Sir Mooray to the gallows. But dinna ye fash yourself aboot it; it will all reet itself in time. Ye're sure o' naething, and ye've got your trust in hand; sae mind it weel, and leave the rest to me.'

Jane responded to this advice by weeping

bitterly over the child, pressing it convulsively to her breast; and in that condition, the next morning, M'Cray left her, and sought the baronet, to find that he had never left the library.

'The puir lassie was half daft last neet, Sir Mooray; but it's a' owre noo, and she's tending the bairn.'

'I wanted you, M'Cray!' exclaimed Sir Murray, the coming of the staunch servitor seeming to rouse him into life. 'I am going to search in one direction: you arrange the men in parties, and leave no place unscoured. Give orders, too, that the great nets be brought out, and let the lake be dragged.'

He shuddered as he spoke these last words, and the gardener turned to go.

'What time is it now?' inquired Sir Murray.

'Just seven of the clock, Sir Mooray,' was

the reply; and then M'Cray took his departure, heedless of the supercilious looks bestowed upon him by one of the footmen, who could not understand what Sir Murray could be thinking about to have that great coarse gardener in the house, and treat him as an equal.

But Sir Murray had placed matters in the right hands. Before half an hour had elapsed parties were organized, consisting of the servants and labourers from the farm close at hand; and a regular search was instituted, the land being methodically gone over—field and forest, bush and ditch. The lake was dragged in every direction, and hour after hour spent, but always with the same result— failure.

There were not wanting those who asserted that my lady must have wandered right away, and the bounds of the search were extended, but still in vain; and at mid-day the parties rested for refreshment, and to determine upon some new plan of action.

Meanwhile, a horse had been brought to the door; and mounting, Sir Murray rode hastily over to the Hall, where, for form's sake, he asked to see Captain Norton, and upon being told of his absence, requested to be shown in to Mrs Norton.

She met him without rising, but sat trembling visibly, as she drew her boy closer to her; for a sense of dread seemed to rob her of the power to move. But a few hours since, and it had been declared to her that this man had tried to poison her cousin, and now he was here. She could not speak, but motioned him to a chair, trying to overcome her weakness, and to meet with fortitude the new misfortune she felt certain was impending.

Sir Murray saw her motion, but he remained standing; and for full five minutes he watched her, with a look mingled of curiosity and compassion.

'Mrs Norton,' he said at last, 'I have come to inflict pain, but I cannot help it. You must judge me leniently when I am gone.'

Ada bowed, and gazed at him with starting eyes.

'One of the Castle servants was here the day before yesterday. Did you see her?'

'I did,' said Ada, huskily.

'She brought a note, did she not, from Lady Gernon?'

'No, Sir Murray.'

'A message?'

'No.'

'She saw Captain Norton?'

'My husband was from home, Sir Murray Gernon.'

'She left a message for him?'

' No.'

' Are you sure? '

' Quite. Your servant came to see me, as your wife's old friend and relative; and, saving the housemaid who admitted her, I alone saw her.'

' Have you any objection to tell me the object of her visit? '

Ada was silent.

'Did she come at the wish of Lady Gernon? '

' No,' said Ada, for she hardly knew what to reply.

' Then you will tell me why she came? '

Ada was still silent.

' Then I will tell you,' said Sir Murray, in a calm voice. ' She came to tell you of some absurd suspicions that she had nursed—to try and convince you that Lady Gernon's life was in danger; for, like the rest of us, she had

been blinded by the treason of a false woman.
I see that the news has not yet reached your
ears. Mrs Norton, your cousin has fled!'

'Fled!' exclaimed Ada, starting to her
feet.

'Yes, fled,' he continued, in measured
tones, as if he were forcing each word from his
lips. 'She left the Castle during my absence,
yesterday afternoon, and she has not returned.
Captain Norton engaged a conveyance yesterday afternoon, and drove away; Captain
Norton has not returned.'

Ada Norton stood, pale as a statue, gazing
at him with lips apart, as she realized his
words, and thought of her husband's absence,
his note, his strange behaviour, and Jane Barker's words respecting the last meeting in the
wood. Her brain reeled, as the thoughts
flashed rapidly through, and for a moment she
felt that she was ready to fall; but she re-

covered herself, to hear that her visitor was still speaking.

'I had a last hope that she might be here —that, overtaken by the storm, this might have been her refuge ; but my hope was faint. Mrs Norton, I might, perhaps, have kept the truth from you for a few hours ; but you must have known it, sooner or later. You have judged me, I believe, very harshly, so far ; now, perhaps, I shall command your pity, as I pity you.'

'Judge you harshly ! Pity you ! You pity me !' exclaimed Ada, flashing into a rage, which lit up her whole countenance, as, with one hand she clutched her boy more tightly to her, and held out the other threateningly at Sir Murray. 'You cold-blooded, cowardly miscreant—you destroyer of the hope and happiness, perhaps the life, of that sweet, suffering woman ! how dare you confront me with your base, clumsily built-up reasoning, as if every woman upon earth possessed your vile, suspicious nature! You dare to come here with your base subterfuges—your das-tardly insinuations—to try and make me be-lieve that Lady Gernon, my pure-hearted cousin, and confidante from a child, has fled with my noble, true, and faithful husband! You lie, you false-hearted dastard—you insidi-ous, courtly, smooth villain—you lie, and you know it! Heaven forgive me my passion, but it is enough to madden me! Go! leave here this instant; for you pollute the place, and you tempt me to believe that you have murdered her! Yes, you may start! But my husband! as true-hearted and honourable a man as ever breathed! How dare you?'

'Woman, where is your husband?' cried Sir Murray, fiercely.

'I do not know. He is from home. How dare you question me?'

'Poor, weak, self-deceiving creature!' he said, contemptuously, 'I do not question you! I have noticed—— Nay, stay here!' he exclaimed, catching her by the wrist. 'You shall hear me! They have been planning long enough now! It was a cursed day when I returned to the Castle; and I soon found that out, though you blinded yourself to the truth. But sooner than have any scandal—than have my name dragged through the Divorce Court, and sneered at by every contemptible fool—I have borne all in silence—suffered, as man never before suffered; and, rejoicing in my weakness, they have corresponded and met! Fool that I was, when I found them last in the wood, and covered the villain—the serpent, the robber of my jewels and of my honour—when

I covered him with my pistol, that I did not shoot him down as one would a common thief and burglar! But, no; I would not have a scandal afloat, even though I was becoming the laughingstock and by-word of my servants! But, there, go! I pity and admire you; for I can feel—you teach me to feel— that there may be yet women worthy of faith!'

As he spoke he threw her hand roughly from him just as the door opened, and Mr and Mrs Elstree entered the room.

'You are here, then!' exclaimed the Rector, in agonized tones. 'We have been to the Castle. In Heaven's name, Murray—Ada— what does all this mean? We hear that Marion is missing! Can you form no idea where she is?'

'Yes!' said Sir Murray, bitterly; 'abroad by this time!'

'What, in Heaven's name, does it all

mean?' exclaimed Mrs Elstree, pitifully.

'Mean, madam!' exclaimed Sir Murray, as he strode to the door, and turned to gaze fiercely at all present—'mean? That I married a harlot!'

138

CHAPTER XXXVIII.

CHANGES AT HAND.

EVERYTHING that could be done in the way of searching was energetically carried out. The lake, every pond, and even many of the water-holes upon the moor were dragged; but no tidings—no trace of Lady Gernon was obtained. M'Cray had seen her walk across the lawn and disappear behind some shrubs, as he was at work, and that seemed to be the last trace. No one could be found who had seen her pass in any direction; and the topic of conversation in Merland village and the neighbourhood began to change its tone, as people learned how Sir Murray had, for a short time, made inquiries respecting the route taken by Captain Norton, pursuing him, too, for some distance, until he seemed to have disappeared, the information he obtained being of a very vague nature.

But it was very plain to those who took an interest in the affair that Sir Murray Gernon's endeavours to trace his lady were made in a half-hearted manner. The search in the neighbourhood of the Castle was strenuous enough, but that was due to the exertions of M'Cray; and when, at the end of a week, people learned that Sir Murray had shut himself up, after discharging half the servants with liberal wages, they raised their eyebrows, and shook their heads, and wondered whether Captain Norton would ever show himself again at the Hall.

As for Jane, she was nearly having a rupture with M'Cray, upon his giving in his adhesion to the popular feeling; but the matter blew over, and whatever might be her thoughts, she said no more, waiting in expectation of the battle that she felt to be in store for her when, rousing himself once more, Sir Murray should recall her words, and wish to discharge her.

But the day she dreaded did not come; while, to the great disgust of the servants, M'Cray seemed to be more and more in the confidence of Sir Murray.

'Why don't he keep to his "gairden," as he calls it?' said the footman, indignantly; for he felt himself much ill-used, since he had to wear his livery, eat his food, and do nothing at all in return, for the baronet's simple meals were taken into his room by M'Cray. Williams, the other footman—Sir

Murray's spy, as Jane indignantly called him —had been amongst the servants first discharged.

'The poor gairden's going to rack and ruin, lassie,' said M'Cray ; 'and just as I was going to make such improvements and alterations ! But Sir Mooray says I'm not to let either of the ither sairvants go to him ; and I believe he frightened that loon in the breeches, because he would take in the letters.'

'But he sha'n't frighten me,' said Jane, firmly. 'I'll never leave the child, come what may.'

'Dinna fash yersel', darling,' said M'Cray, tenderly. 'I've got the wages and orders of six more that are to be sent away at once, but ye're nae one of them. Sir Mooray winna discharge ye till he packs me off.'

'Indeed !' said Jane. 'And how do you know ? '

'Why, we've been talking aboot ye, lassie; and Sir Mooray said he had made up his mind to go abroad again, and asked me if I'd gang wi' him; and though it cut me to the heart to leave my fruit and flowers, lassie, I thocht I'd see new sorts in the far countree, and I said I'd gang.'

'It didn't fret you, then, to think of leaving me?' said Jane, bitterly.

'Hoot, lassie! and who's aboot to gang and leave ye?' exclaimed M'Cray. 'Sir Mooray said I was to see and get a good nurse to tak' charge of the bairn—one as would go abroad; and 1 telled him he couldna do better than keep ye, when I thocht he was going to fly at me. But I telled him, quite still like, that we'd promised to marry, and that if he didna tak' ye, lassie, he wadna tak' me; and that seemed to make him mad for a bit, till I telled him that ye lo'ed weel the bairn, and that ye were a gude girl at heart. But he wadna listen.'

' Was it to be a good place, Alexander ? ' said Jane.

' Ay, lassie; I was to have a fair bit o' siller.'

' Then you mustn't give it up for me.'

' I didna mean to, lassie,' said M'Cray, coolly.

Jane was piqued, and said nothing.

' There, lassie, I winna beat aboot the bush any more. It was settled at last that we twain are to gang thegither; and I agreed for both, and Sir Mooray starts next week for the Lake Como.'

' And like you ! ' said Jane, with asperity. ' How could you know that I'd go ? '

' Why, didn't I ken that ye'd gang for my sake ? ' said M'Cray.

' No, indeed ! ' exclaimed Jane.

'That's just what I thocht,' said M'Cray, with a twinkle in his eye; 'but I was quite sure ye would on account of the bairn.'

Jane smiled, in spite of herself, as M'Cray's arm was passed round her; but her eyes filled with tears directly after, as she placed the child upon a chair, and then went down upon her knees before it, kissing it again and again.

'It was good, and kind, and thoughtful of you, Alexander,' she said, turning to the gardener; 'and I know you've been having a hard battle for me.'

'Weel, lassie, he did want a deal o' pruning, certainly,' said M'Cray.

'But I'm very—very grateful!' sobbed Jane, 'for the poor child seems all one has to live for now!'

'All, lassie?' said M'Cray, dryly.

'Well, no; not all,' said Jane. 'But I'm not worthy of you, and I never ought to have made you the promise I did, for I can't love you as much as you ought to be loved.'

'Hoot, lassie!' cried M'Cray, kneeling by her side, and drawing her to him, 'gin ye try like that, I'm quite satisfied, for what more need a man wush for, than for his couthie wee bodie to try and love him with all her heart?'

146

CHAPTER XXXIX.

MR CHUNT'S TOAST.

MR CHUNT presided over a good many discussions in his parlour, where farmer and tradesman met to talk over the course of events during the first few weeks. The subject of Lady Gernon's disappearance was tabooed by general consent. It was not the first event of the kind that had happened through badly-assorted marriages, and wouldn't be the last, said the baker, sententiously ; and then it was acknowledged· by general consent that money didn't make happiness, and that there was a deal of wickedness in this world.

Upon another night Mr Chunt took to bewailing in public the injury done to his trade, by the shutting up of the Castle.

'Looks a reg'lar devastation, gentlemen,' he said; 'things all in holland, shutters closed, stables locked up, and all just as if it didn't belong to nobody.'

'Oh, Sir Murray will be back one of these days,' said a small farmer, cheerfully, 'and then trade will brighten up again; meanwhile, you must be contented with our custom, Chunt. He'll tire of foreign parts, you'll see.'

'Don't hear any likelihood of Mrs Norton going, I suppose?' said one.

'Not she, poor little woman; she even looks quite cheerful, and is always out with that little boy of hers. Noble little chap he grows!'

'Ah!' said another, 'he played his cards

well, the Captain did. He hadn't been gone long before there was two couples down to arrest him—two parties, one after the other. Stopped here, they did. Post-chaises : come down in style. Didn't they, Chunt?'

The landlord nodded in confirmation.

'Just got away in time. Pity, though. He'd have been a bonny man if it hadn't been for his disappointment, and those iron shares. It was on account of his being director, and answerable for a good deal, I suppose, that the bailiffs wanted him.'

A week passed, and then Chunt, who had been waiting to have a good full audience, brought out a large auctioneer's posting bill, and laid it before his customers as a surprise.

'What d'yer think of that, gentlemen, eh?' he said. 'Merland will be another place soon. There's poor old Gurdon and poor old Barker both dead within the last four-and-twenty hours, and now that's been sent to me to stick up in the bar. Read it out, Mr Mouncey.'

The baker put on his spectacles, and read aloud the list of the 'elegant and superior household furniture and effects, to be sold by auction, without reserve, at Merland Rectory, by direction of the Reverend Henry Elstree, who was leaving the place.'

'Chunt's about right,' said Huttoft, the saddler: 'the place won't be the same, soon. The old people at the Rectory ain't looked the same, since I saw them coming back that day from the Hall—the day after Lady Gernon elop—disappeared.'

'Well, gentlemen,' said the landlord, 'I believe I'm as sorry as any one present; but it's no use to fret for other folks' troubles. I propose that we have glasses round of brandy hot, gentlemen, for I feel quite sinking.'

'Do you pay, Chunt?' said Mouncey, jocosely.

'There ain't a man present as would be more free, gentlemen,' said the landlord, 'if I could ; but, I put it to the company, with the present fall off in my trade, am I able ?'

'No—no!' was chorused ; and, the glasses being filled, Jonathan Chunt proposed a toast which was drunk with acclamation, and the landlord's toast was :

'Gentlemen, here's to happier times!'

END OF BOOK I.

BOOK II.—SECOND GENERATION.

CHAPTER I.

AFTER TWENTY YEARS.

'YOU dog! you confounded lubber! Drive on, or you'll have them out of sight!' shouted a frank, opened-faced young fellow of some three or four and twenty, as he leaned out of the front window of a post-chaise, and urged his post-boy to increase of speed.

'An' how can I get another mile an hour out on such bastes, yer honner?' said the post-boy in answer. 'The crayture I'm riding takes no more heed of the spur than the grate baste the levvyathan of Howly Scripture; and as to the blind mare there, the more I larrup her the more she hangs back out ov the collar.'

'Gammon !—nonsense !' cried the young man : ' you can catch them if you like.'

'Shure, sor, I'd catch 'em if it was me. The spirit of me's been close alongside this last quarter of an hour ; but the bastes here 'ave got skins like a rhinosros.'

'Half a guinea if you catch them and go by in the next two miles,' shouted the traveller.

'An' why didn't ye spake sooner, sor ? It's meself's the boy to get it out of the bastes if it's to be done at all ; ' and the effect of the golden spur was soon visible in the way in which the mire of the cross-country road flew up from the whirling wheels.

For a couple of hours now, with the present and the preceding post-boy, had this chase been carried on,—now one chaise, now the other, being to the fore; the explanation of this being of the simplest character.

Lieutenant Brace Norton, of H.M.S. 'Icarus,' had just arrived in port, and was, as he put it, homeward bound after his first voyage with the rank of lieutenant. In fact, he took so much pride in his epaulette, won after no end of midshipman's adventures, that, until better sense prevailed, he had had some thought of wearing it home. He had travelled as far as the county town by rail, and now, having a rather large idea of his own importance, was finishing his journey in one of the post-chaises—scarce things then—left upon the road. At the railway station he had twice encountered a fair young face, small, dark, oval, and with a pair of sad-looking, lustrous eyes, their owner leaning upon the arm of a tall, gray-haired gentleman ; and after making his way to the hotel and ordering his conveyance, spending the time consumed in getting it ready by smoking a cigar, he was startled, upon going to the door to lounge about the steps, by seeing the same travellers take their places in a chaise which had been prepared before his own.

'Do you know who that gentleman is ?' he had said to the landlord, who had bowed his visitors to the door.

'Can't say, sir, I'm sure,' was the reply. 'Please excuse me, sir—I'm wanted.'

'Here waiter, my chaise; look sharp!' exclaimed the young lieutenant, slipping a shilling into the man's hand, on seeing the direction the first chaise had taken. 'Hurry them on, there's a good fellow, and tell them to put in the best pair of horses.'

'Best pair's gone, sir, with number one chaise, but I'll get them to look alive.'

In spite of his stamping with impatience, and conducting himself in a most unreasonable manner, even to going into the yard himself, and hoisting the sluggish post-boy—a youth of about sixty—into his jacket, a full quarter of an hour elapsed before the chaise began to rattle out of the yard with the traveller in it.

'Here—hi! stop!' shouted a voice, as they turned down the main street.

'What the deuce now?' exclaimed the traveller, as the post-boy pulled up, after nearly running into a flock of sheep, and the waiter came panting up.

'Please, sir, you ain't paid for the cigar, and sherry and biscuit,' exclaimed the man, in injured tones.

'Confound it, no!' cried the young man. 'And—I say, I haven't got my portmanteau!

There, my man, look sharp, whatever you do ! '

Five minutes more elapsed, but at length the bill was paid, the portmantcau secured to the front, and the crazy vehicle was once more well under weigh, the young sailor fuming the while with impatience. But as soon as the town was passed, liberal promises sent the shabby cattle scuffling along at a pretty good pace ; and when the traveller had about given up all hopes of again seeing the face that had attracted his attention, the first post-chaise became visible, slowly crawling up one of the hills about half-way between Lincoln and Marshton, when again urging on the post-boy, the vehicle was at length overtaken, and whilst passing it the young man's heart leaped as he again caught sight of the fair traveller, leaning forward to see who was passing, but withdrawing instantly upon seeing that she was the object of attention.

Twice did Brace Norton find the oppor-
tunities for a short glance at the now averted
face: once during the stages, and again when
they changed horses at Marshton; but now,
to his disgust, it seemed that he had been
favoured with worse cattle than before; and in
spite of his urging the fresh post-boy—a
native of 'Sorrey,' as he took an opportunity of
assuring his employer—it seemed that he was
to be left entirely at the rear, to see the face
no more.

But the golden spur prevailed; and as
the young lieutenant saw that they were
gaining rapidly, he threw himself back,
muttering,

'What a thing it is that there are no
women at sea! It only wants their presence
to make it perfect. I wonder who those can
be, though? On a visit somewhere. Jove!
What luck if it's anywhere near us!'

His reverie was interrupted by the broadly-speaking post-boy yoho-ing to the one in front, and the next minute they passed the first chaise in an easy canter; but Brace Norton obtained no view, for, to his great chagrin, the window on this side—the side occupied by the gentleman—had the blind drawn down.

'Didn't I do it in style, yer honner?' cried the post-boy, turning in his saddle to grin.

'Yes—yes; but easy now. Let them pass you.' And then to himself the traveller muttered, 'I shall be right next time.'

'Is that to be included in the half-guinea, yer honner?' cried the post-boy, with a leer; but he obtained no answer, save a fierce gesture not to look back; for now the passing was to be performed by the other chaise, which in a few moments had again left them behind, while this time again the susceptible sailor had been doomed to disappointment, for as the chaise passed, the momentary glance showed him that the lady occupant's head was averted, and that she was talking to her companion.

' But what a neck ! ' muttered the young man ; ' and what glorious hair ! What a cluster of braids ! Why, she could sit on it, I'd swear, if it were down. Confound you ! will you go on ? ' he shouted, thrusting his head from the window. ' What are you crawling like that for ? '

' Did yer honner want me to be always passing them, widout ever letting them get first again ? ' said the post-boy.

' You blundering idiot ! ' muttered the young man, laughing in spite of himself. ' Drive on, Pat,' he said, aloud, ' and pass them again.'

' Me name's Jeames, yer honner, av ye

please,' said the post-boy, with dignity, and for a short distance he drove sulkily on at a very moderate pace, till the thought that he had not yet obtained the promised half-guinea prompted him to try and keep his employer in a good temper; and once more he passed the foremost chaise at a canter, slackening again in obedience to orders received soon afterwards.

Now every one who has been much upon the road must be fully aware that there is a feeling existent amply shared by man and horse, which, however strange the comparison may seem, is fully expressed in the old saying, that most people like to play first fiddle. Be driving, and pass the sorriest old jaded brute that was ever verging upon the cat's-meat barrow, and see if the poor beast does not, for a few minutes, prick up his ears, and break into a trot to regain his place. Generally the driver is ready enough to urge him on, and if you slacken pace for a few minutes, ten to one but you are passed in your turn.

It was so here with the post-boy and horses of the other chaise : to be passed here on the road again and again by a rival was not to be borne; and the slackening under Brace Norton's instructions being taken as a signal of defeat, there soon came a shout from behind to the Irish boy to draw aside, one which, being rather sulky at having had a mistake made in his country, the post-boy refused to heed; and just as Brace was hopefully gazing from his window for another glance, there came the crash of wheel against wheel, the swerving aside of the horses, and in less time than it can be written, to Brace Norton's horror, he saw the vehicle of his companions of the road overturned—the off-

wheels in the ditch, and one horse kicking
and plunging in a way that threatened death
to the occupants of the carriage.

CHAPTER II.

THE WRECK ASHORE.

'YE'VE done it now, sor, an' I hope ye're satisfied!' said James, sitting complacently on his saddle, and looking at the plunging horses, his fellow-servant with one leg entangled in the harness, and the havoc made at each plunge of the uppermost beast.

'You scoundrel!' exclaimed Brace, furiously, as he leaped down. 'Why didn't. you give more room? Here, come and help!'

'Can't lave me bastes, sor, or they'd take fright, they're so full of sperrit,' said the youth, coolly, as, running to the prostrate chaise, Brace contrived to drag open the door, feeling, as he did so, that he was alone to blame for the accident.

'Here, quick! my child! help her first,' exclaimed the gentleman, but most needlessly, for the young man had neither look nor thought for him, but was striving to lift the insensible and bleeding form of the wounded girl from the wreck. For at the first crash of the overturning chaise the window had been driven in, and one of the splinters of glass had gashed her temple.

'Good Heavens! what have I done?' muttered Brace, as he succeeded in passing his arms round the senseless form, lifted it by main force from the door, and then bore it to the grass a few yards further on, where, laying it down, he proceeded to press his handkerchief to the wound.

'Let me come, young man,' said a harsh voice at his elbow, and, starting with surprise, Brace saw that the gentleman, till now forgotten, had climbed from the chaise, and now made no scruple in thrusting him aside to take his place.

'What can I do? Had I not better gallop off for a doctor?'

'Thank you, no,' was the cold reply, as the gentleman, for an instant, looked the tenderer of service full in the face. 'This is no scene from a romance, sir. You need trouble yourself no further. My daughter is more frightened than hurt, I dare say.'

'A cold-hearted, unfeeling brute,' muttered Brace to himself, for he was greatly excited, and felt at that moment as if he would have given the world to have been allowed to kneel there and support the inanimate form. For a moment he felt ready to make confession that

he had been the cause of the accident, but
that he felt would be folly; and once more,
heedless of the cold reception his offers met
with, he proposed that a doctor should be
fetched.

'If I required a medical man, sir,' said the
gentleman, 'there is the post-boy, my paid
servant, that I could send for one: unless,' he
said, tauntingly, 'you, sir, wish to earn something more than my thanks.'

The colour rose to the young man's cheek
as he met the cold, glittering eye turned to
him for a moment; but he smothered the re-
sentment he could not avoid feeling, and, without a word, turned away to a clear part of the
ditch, returning, in a few minutes, with his
navy cloth cap half full of water.

The gentleman frowned as he saw this
favour forced upon him as he thought, and
unwillingly accepting it, he sprinkled the white

face, and bathed the forehead, wiping away the ruddy stains, and binding a handkerchief tightly across the wound. But for awhile there were no signs of returning animation, and once more, in spite of the scowl upon the father's face, Brace Norton hurried away to bring more water.

'There is a faint shade of colour returning now,' exclaimed Brace, eagerly.

' Then perhaps you will have the goodness to retire, sir,' said the gentleman, haughtily. ' My daughter is not accustomed to the society of strangers; and, at such a time, your presence would be a fresh shock.'

' But this is a lonely place, sir. You are miles away from any aid. Pray let me endeavour to be of some service. Surely I can help you.'

' I thank you, no,' was the cold reply.

' But for the lady's sake, sir,' exclaimed

Brace, almost indignantly. 'You will take my chaise, and continue your journey?'

'Young man,' was the rude answer, 'I am not in the habit of placing myself under obligations to strangers. I shall not require your chaise: I have no doubt, with the help of some of the labourers about, our own vehicle can be set right in a very short time.'

'Sure, sor, the short time will be a month,' said Brace's post-boy; 'the hint wheel's off intirely, and Jerry Stone siz as the harness is all to tatthers, an' he wants to know if aither of ye gentlemen have got a drop of brandy wid ye, for the poor boy feels faint.'

In effect, the other post-boy was seated upon a bank beside his now extricated horses —set free by the liberal use of a knife amongst the harness; and it was evident, from the way in which the poor fellow was rocking himself to and fro, that he was in great pain; while a glance at the wretched chaise showed the impossibility of making use of it for further proceeding upon that day.

But Brace Norton possessed something of the irrepressible in his composition, and, speaking gently, he said, addressing the late speaker:

'I am aware, sir, that it is unpleasant to have favours forced upon you by a complete stranger, but let me beg of you not to let the little I offer be looked upon in the light of a favour. For the young lady's sake, pray make use of my chaise, and leave me to take my chance. I dare not presume to offer you advice, but would not a reference to some medical man be advisable? This long-continued swoon——'

Brace Norton said no more, for, glancing from father to daughter as he spoke, he became aware that sensibility had returned, and that a pair of soft, sad, dreamy eyes were fixed

upon him, but only for their lids to be lowered,
and a faint blush to overspread the pallid
cheeks upon her seeing that her gaze was ob-
served.

'Do you feel in pain?' said the gentleman,
bending over her, but paying no heed to Brace
Norton's remarks.

'No, papa; only a little faint. But you
are not hurt?'

'No, no; not at all.' Then, in an un-
dertone: 'How very unfortunate!' and he
frowned at the shattered chaise as he would
have done at its driver.

Brace Norton was wise enough in his
generation to see that the less he said the less
likely he would be to give offence; but a bitter feeling of disappointment came over him
as he found how completely his presence was
ignored.

'If it were not for that sweet girl he might

walk,' muttered the young man ; but the next moment his heart leaped with pleasure, when, after standing thoughtfully for a few moments, and then glancing from his daughter to the wreck and back again, the gentleman spoke somewhat more courteously.

'Necessity forces me, sir, to accept the offer of your chaise for my—for reasons of my own,' he added, hastily. 'I will make use of it on condition that you allow me to pay any—'

'Good heavens, sir !' exclaimed Brace, as haughtily now as the stranger, 'give me credit for wishing to act as should one gentleman towards another whom he sees with his jibboom —absurd !—whom he encounters in distress —I beg pardon, I mean in—in a strait,' exclaimed Brace, desperately, for his nautical imagery did not find much favour. 'I am only a simple officer in the navy, and no doubt a sea life makes me somewhat rude, but my offers of service are genuine, not mercenary.'

The stranger bowed, and turned to his daughter, who was now standing at his side.

'Take down that portmanteau,' exclaimed Brace to the post-boy.

'Yes, sor!' And after a good deal of grunting, unbuckling, and lifting it was placed by the road side.

'If you will allow me,' said Brace, 'I will see that the damaged chaise is sent back to its owner.'

He turned then to hand the lady into the vehicle, but he was motioned back; not, though, without receiving from her a faint smile of thanks.

'My daughter needs no assistance further than I can render,' was the stern response to Brace's offer. 'Your handkerchief, sir!'

Brace took the handkerchief handed to

him, as if the donor were about to strike him down. Then he drew back as father and daughter entered the chaise, so that he did not catch the order given to the post-boy. Then there was a stiff salutation from the gentleman; a slight bow from the lady; and the horses had started, leaving Brace, bare-headed, handsome, and flushed, standing in the road, till, suddenly the front windows were dashed down, the door partly opened, and, evidently suffering from some strong emotion, the face of the gentleman appeared to be turned the next moment towards the post-boy, as he roared, in a voice of thunder:

'Stop!'

CHAPTER III.

ANOTHER ENCOUNTER.

'WHAT now?' grumbled the post-boy, as he turned in his saddle, and then, in obedience to the gesticulations directed at him, pulled up very slowly, and not until he had traversed nearly a hundred yards of road. Flinging down the steps, the gentleman alighted, half dragged his daughter from her seat, so rudely, indeed, that she nearly fell. Then drawing her arm tightly through his own, he walked back to the injured post-boy and gave some order, his forehead netted the while with the swelling veins, and his face now pale and flushed by the passion that agitated his breast.

He seemed to quite ignore the presence of Brace, and before the young man could recover from his astonishment, father and daughter were hurriedly walking away.

'Is there anything wrong?—is—that is, can I be of no assistance?' stammered Brace, as he ran after and overtook them—speaking to the father, but gazing the while in the daughter's pale and frightened face, as if his eyes were riveted there; but only to meet with a strange, imploring look, half horror—half dread.

The stranger tried to speak, as he raised one trembling hand, pointing towards the carriage, but no words passed his lips; and motioning the young man fiercely, he hurriedly led his trembling charge away.

'Is he mad?' said Brace to himself. 'And to drag that poor girl away like that! What more can I do?' he muttered, as the post-boy drew up along-side of where he stood.

'I've put the portmanty back in the front, sor, as them two ain't agoing.'

But Brace Norton did not seem to hear him, as, seeking for some clue to this strange alteration in the old man's behaviour, his eyes fell upon the seat of the chaise the travellers had so lately occupied, where, forgotten for the time, lay his travelling writing-case, with its brass-plate bearing his name and that of his ship.

Well, yes, he had forgotten that, but what was there in his name to make the old man leap from the chaise as if half mad, unless—

There was a faint suspicion in his mind— a dim and confused mingling of fragments of old stories that had never made any impression upon him before ; but now he struggled hard to recall in their entirety these shadowy memories of the past. In vain, though ; he only grew more mystified than ever. The strangers were already at a turn of the road, and it was in his mind to run after them and ask for some explanation, when his eyes fell upon the handkerchief that the gentleman had placed within his hands—a handkerchief that now for the first time he saw was not the one he had applied to the injured temple, and his heart throbbed as he thought that it was his that she now held; but the next instant a feeling of trouble and pleasure mingled, as it were, came upon him, and he looked eagerly in the corner of the piece of cambric, to find there, in faint but still legible characters, the two words, 'Isa Gernon.'

An old quarrel—some unpleasantry be-

tween the two families—some feeling of bitter-
ness on the part of Sir Murray Gernon, who,
with his daughter, had been resident in Italy
for some twenty years. That must be it,
for he could evoke nothing from the past—
nothing tangible. Sir Murray had seen, then,
the name of Norton in the chaise, and he refused to accept service from any one bearing
that patronymic. It was absurd, too, after all
these years; but it would only be an insult to
a man of such pride of speech and mien to
follow and press upon him what he would look
upon as a favour. A little gentle advance or
two upon the part of those at the Hall might
put all right; for if that was Sir Murray
Gernon returned unexpectedly after all these
years to dwell at the Castle, there must be
no enmity now. And this, then, was his
daughter!

So mused Brace Norton as he mentally

smoothed away all difficulties ahead, rejoicing, too, he knew not why, at the prospect of possessing such neighbours. He must, he felt, question them at home about the past, and try to adopt means for a reconciliation.

Here he stopped short, roused by the sight of the wrecked chaise, and recalling the position of those from whom he had but now parted. If that were Sir Murray Gernon, he was a good six miles from the Castle, to which place it seemed impossible that he could walk. What could be done, then, to help them without its being known from whence the help arrived ?

He had at last determined upon being taken back to the town, and informing the hotel-keeper of the state of affairs, when a heavily-laden fly was driven up, the roof and the driver's box being filled with luggage, when, seeing the state of the post-boy and the

injured chaise, the fly-man pulled up, and began to make inquiries.

'No bones broke, Tommy,' said the post-
boy, in reply; 'but I shall be precious glad
to get back.'

'An' was that the chay Sir Mooray Jair-
non was in?' exclaimed a voice; and a
massive-looking grizzled head was thrust out
of the fly window.

'Was it your master,' said the post-boy:
'gray gent with a young lady?'

'Yes—yes! Where are they?' exclaimed
an eager female voice.   'Pray get out, M'Cray,
and see.'

'Dinna fash yersel', lassie,' said the first
speaker.   'There's naebodie hurt, I ken.
But where's Sir Mooray, my lad?'

'Walked on,' said the post-boy.

'You are, then, that gentleman's servant?'

exclaimed Brace Norton, now eagerly joining in the conversation.

'And wha may ye be that ask sic a question?'

'Only a traveller on the road,' said Brace, smiling, as he glanced at the comely, pleasant-faced female who had just stepped out of the fly; 'but your master and the young lady have just walked on. You have arrived in capital time, for I fear that she is much shaken. It was a very rude fall.'

'Gudeness save us, Jenny! jump in again, and let's drive on. I'm verra grateful for your information, sir, and I thank ye.'

'Pray make haste, M'Cray!' cried the pleasant-faced dame, smoothing back the gray-streaked bands of hair from her forehead.

And the next minute, with the satisfaction of knowing that he had sent help where it was

needed, Brace Norton was standing alone in
the road.

He was very thoughtful and serious as he
stood there, once more trying to bring back
something of the old history from the past
days of his parents' life; but he soon gave it
up as an impossible task, and one most
unsuited for his present place of study. So,
assisting the injured post-boy to mount, upon
his reiterated assurance that he could easily
reach home alone, Brace once more stepped
up to his own conveyance, and, very thoughtful and dreamy, slowly continued his journey.

Four miles further on, having purposely
kept the post-boy at a slow rate, Brace overtook the late occupants of the fly, arm-in-arm,
and sturdily trudging on towards Merland,
when, rightly concluding that their places had
been taken by Sir Murray and his daughter,

Brace stopped the post-boy, and invited the old Scot and his companion to share the conveyance.

'Na, na, sir; ye're verra kind, but I'd raither not, and the gudewife here is of the same opinion. I wish ye a gude day, sir —a gude day. Ye'll excuse our hurrying on.'

There was a something in the man's manner that whispered of exclusiveness, and a desire to avoid strangers, which checked Brace Norton in his desire to press his offers of service. He had the good sense to feel, too, that, with the master so determinedly distant, any advances toward the servant might be looked upon as an insult. So, reluctantly giving the order to proceed, the wheels of the chaise spun round, and the next moment, at a turn of the road, Brace caught a glimpse of the couple trudging along; when, throwing himself back in the vehicle, the young man began to ponder upon what was the cause, his thoughts, too, often being occupied by the faces of his mother and Isa Gernon.

CHAPTER IV.

DREAD.

TWENTY winters had not come and passed away without leaving traces of their frosty rime upon the heads of Captain Norton and his wife; but as they stood in the Hall dining-room, hand clasping hand, and gazing into each other's face, it was evident that, whatever might have been the past, there was peace, content, and happiness there.

'Yes,' said Mrs Norton, now grown into a pleasant matronly dame, ' he has come back.

The whole village rings with the news. So unexpected, too.'

'Poor fellow!' said Captain Norton, after a few minutes' quiet thought. 'Heaven grant that he may be more happy! I am sorry, though, Ada—very sorry; for his coming seems to open old wounds. But come—come, darling!' he exclaimed, as he drew her towards his breast. 'Don't wear that troubled face. Surely, after all these years—'

'Pray forgive me!' said Mrs Norton, nestling closer to him; and she smiled happily in reply to his caresses. 'As you say, Philip, Heaven help him, and clear up the dark mystery of his life! I do not see why we should trouble ourselves about his coming back.'

'Well—no,' said Captain Norton, uneasily; 'but one cannot help recalling how events shaped themselves after his last return. But there, let us dismiss it all, for I cannot trust myself even now to dwell upon all these old matters. I would make up my mind to leave, and at once, in spite of the inconvenience, only that it would be like a tacit acknowledgment that I was afraid to meet him; and you know how charitable people can be.'

'Oh no; we could not think of leaving,' said Mrs Norton, hastily; 'but I think—nay, I feel sure that with him the past will be buried entirely; for, Philip,' she added, solemnly, 'may Heaven forgive me if I am uncharitable, but I believe that the man who could so cruelly malign my husband must have had his own ends to serve. I could not refrain from saying this, as the subject was brought up; but whatever evil—whatever wrong-doing was connected with poor Marion's disappearance, must some day or other be brought out into the light of day. Twenty years—twenty long years—has the matter slumbered, and it may slumber twenty more; and, in spite now of my utter indifference to public opinion, I cannot help longing for the mystery to be cleared up in our day. But, whether or no, promise me this, dearest, that it shall not be allowed to trouble you—that you will not brood over it; and that, come what may, you will avoid all encounter with that bad, proud man, whose coming seems like a cloud sent over dear old Merland. I almost feel thankful that poor Mr and Mrs Elstree are now far away from trouble and care. There was that dread suspicion, though, in both their hearts; I feel sure, however, they struggled to the last to keep it back. But there: let us dismiss it all; and you promise me, do you not?'

Captain Norton's calm, quiet smile was enough to reassure his wife; and as he took his seat at a side-table, covered with correspondence, she stood behind him, leaning her hands upon his shoulder.

'We are going on at a famous rate, Ada,' he said, after a busy pause, in short, sharp, decisive tones, that smacked of the man of business—'returns increasing every month. Some of the prophetic old wiseacres would give their ears now for shares in our rusty old iron company. By the way, though, Brace has not written for any money lately. Is it not time we heard from him?'

'Yes,' said Mrs Norton, with anxiety in her tones; 'and—'

'Now, don't be an old fidget,' said the Captain, laughingly, as once more he drew her towards him. 'That poor old head of yours is as full of shipwrecks and disasters at sea as one of the wreck-charts or Lloyd's ledgers. What a pity it is that we did not have half-a-dozen boys for you to share that weak old heart of yours amongst, so that you need not have had to worry yourself to death about one!'

'But surely we ought to have had a letter a month since.'

'Certainly, my love, if the poor boy had had a post-office close at hand into which he could pop it. Don't be so unreasonable. You don't know how even an adverse wind will keep a vessel away from port for weeks together. You must study statistics, so as to ease that heart of yours, by learning how seldom a mishap befalls a ship. We shall be hearing from him before long, and— There, bless my soul, I must keep a clerk; I've forgotten to answer Harrison and Son's letter.'

'What was that about?' said Mrs Norton, as, pleased to see how happy her husband was in his business pursuits—upon which, in spite of adversity at the outset, fortune had of late smiled in full sunshine—she tried to enter into each matter, knowing full well how his busy life had been the cure for a mind diseased.

'What was it about?' said Captain Norton, dreamily. 'Oh, about the marsh—the warping, you know. I am to have two thousand acres.'

'But I don't know,' said Mrs Norton, smiling; 'you promised to explain.'

'To be sure; so I did!' he exclaimed, eagerly reaching down a rolled-up plan, and spreading it upon the table. 'Now look here, Ada; this will be an expensive affair, and we shall reap no benefit from it ourselves, for it is a matter of years and years; but that young dog will have an estate which will make him hold up his head as high as he likes. Now, see here—this is my side. I've bought these two thousand acres of worthless marsh-land—worthless save for peat-digging and wild-duck shooting. This is the piece, Ada, love,' he said, solemnly, as he laid a finger upon the plan. ' I chose this so that I might preserve the pine wood untouched.'

He stopped to gaze up in his wife's face, and as she recalled the past, she bent over him until her cheek touched his forehead.

' Well, love,' he said, raising himself and speaking cheerfully, ' we—that is to say, the other purchasers and myself—dig a large drain, or canal, through our marsh pieces right to the Trent, and fit our drain with sluice-gates, so that at every high tide we flood our low tract of marsh with the thick, muddy waters loaded with the alluvial soil of York-shire and our own county, brought down by many a river and stream, which, after the fashion of the hill floods, by slow and almost imperceptible degrees, is deposited upon our peat and rushes, in a heavy, unctuous, wondrously rich mud, or warp, till, in the course of time, we have it two, three, and in places even four feet deep. Then comes the change: we cease flooding, and give all our attention to thoroughly draining our warp land, which now becomes, in place of marsh, fit only to grow water-plants, a rich and fertile soil. Nature has converted it for us; and twenty years hence, instead of marsh, Master Brace will have a couple of thousand acres of the best soil in England. That is all I can do for him, and after all I don't think that it will be such a very mean heritage. Now, love, what do you say to that?'

Mrs Norton's answer was a cry of joy: for at that moment, free of step, bright and happy, in came Brace Norton, to be strained again and again to his mother's breast.

There was a grim smile of pride and pleasure upon Captain Norton's scarred face, as, after hastily rolling up his plans, he caught at his son's disengaged hand.

'My dear Brace, how well and hearty you look!' he exclaimed, as he scanned the broad chest and muscular limbs of his son.

'Well?   Ay! father, never better,' was the reply. 'And I don't know that I ever saw you look better.'

'Oh! I'm well enough,' said Captain Norton. 'But, my dear boy, what a pity it is that you did not join our service! With that build of yours, you would have drilled as upright as a dart.'

'And broken my heart over the pipe-clay, eh, father?' laughed the young man. 'I'm right enough—make a tolerable sailor, perhaps, but I should have been a poor soldier. But, I say,' said Brace, after half-an-hour's questioning and answering, ' I have had quite an adventure coming over: came across a fine, fierce, gray old fellow, with—oh! mamma, the most lovely girl you ever saw in your life ! '

' Pooh ! ' laughed the Captain, ' the sailor's Poll. What asses you boys do make of yourselves ! '

' All right, father ; only let me bray in peace.'

' Fell in love at first sight, and would have eloped, only the fierce, gray old fellow was watchful as a dragon, eh, Brace ? ' said Captain Norton, smiling.

' Belay, there, will you ! ' cried Brace. ' How can I go on with my story ? Not quite so fast as that. But there, sir, we can spare you for the present. I'm talking to some one here who can sympathize. Really, you know,' he continued, passing his arm round his mother's waist, as she gazed at him fondly, and drawing her to the window, 'she was about the sweetest girl I ever set eyes on. Quite an adventure : chaises passing; theirs overset; sweet girl's temple cut; insensible; offering aid; received very haughtily by the old gentleman—quite a Spanish grandee ! '

Ada Norton started, as those words seemed to carry her back five-and-twenty years, and the smile upon her lips slowly faded away.

' Well,' continued Brace, lightly, ' I spoiled my cap by fetching water in it from a pool, like a true knight-errant would have done with his casque, and bound up the bleeding temple with my handkerchief. Then, after a great deal of snubbing from the old gentle-man, I was rewarded by a sweet smile of thanks from the lady as I prevailed upon the Don to take my chaise and come on. Got them in at last, after a great deal of ceremoni-ous fencing, and they drove off, but only to stop directly. Old gentleman leaps out, drags sweet girl after him, and goes raging off; and all, I suppose, because he had seen my name upon my leather writing-case; while, for explanation, I have the young lady's handkerchief, bearing the sweet name of Isa Gernon. But, good heavens, my dear mother, how pale you look! Father, what is the matter?'

Captain Norton had risen from his seat and advanced to his wife, who, pale as death, stood gazing at him with a terrified expression upon her countenance.

'My dear father, what does all this mean?' exclaimed Brace, with real anxiety in his tones. 'What mystery is there here? Of course I concluded that the elderly gentleman was Sir Murray Gernon; and I have some misty recollections of an old family quarrel, and Lady Gernon running away. There, I have arrived

at my cable's end.   What is it all?   I trust
nothing wrong.'

'Speak to him, Ada!' cried Captain Norton, hoarsely.   'There must be no more of
this!'

And without another word he hurried from
the room; while, perfectly astounded, Brace
turned to his mother for some explanation of
what was to him a profound mystery.

CHAPTER V.

ON THE BYGONE.

'AND where had my father been at the time?' said Brace Norton, after sitting with knitted brows listening to his mother's narrative of the past.

'France—abroad—to avoid arrest; for his affairs in connection with the mine were then in a sad state. It was his absence which made matters wear so suspicious an aspect.'

'Suspicious? Yes,' said Brace, angrily, 'suspicious enough to base minds! How long was he away?'

'Five, nearly six, months,' said Mrs Norton.

'But you never believed this charge, mother? You never thought my father guilty?'

'Guilty? No!' exclaimed Mrs Norton, proudly. 'Your father, Brace, is the soul of honour, and above suspicion; but matters shaped themselves most cruelly against him.'

'That Gurdon must have had the cross,' said Brace, after a thoughtful pause; 'and you say that he obtained his deserts—transported?'

Mrs Norton nodded her head.

'But Lady Gernon's disappearance—what could have become of her? Was it possible that she was deluded away out of revenge— perhaps with the cross for a bait—by some one or other of Gurdon's associates, so that she fell into some trap?'

'My son—my dear boy, pray do not talk of it any more,' said Mrs Norton, sadly. 'It is a rock upon which our happiness was nearly wrecked; but avoid it now. It was right that you should know all after the strange meeting of to-day; but you see now the reason for your father's—for my agitation, and for the strong emotion displayed by Sir Murray Gernon. It is quite impossible, as you must see, that the old intimacy should be renewed. Your father's —my peace of mind depends upon our keeping at a distance—upon the past, Brace, being deeply buried. You see that I am speaking freely—that I am keeping nothing back, in order that you may be upon your guard, and do nothing to endanger the happiness of what, my child, has been these many years a happy home.'

'But,' exclaimed Brace, impetuously, 'if the mystery could be cleared up! I do not like that, even with Sir Murray Gernon, there should be a doubt of my father's honour.'

'Brace, my dear boy,' said Mrs Norton, laying her hand upon the young man's arm, 'let the past rest; it is a subject that has brought white hairs into more than one head. It has been thought upon till left in despair. I pray to be forgiven if I am unjust, but I do not think that Sir Murray Gernon entertains a single suspicion against your father, whatever he may once have felt. Time must have removed old impressions; but for his own black conduct—— There, I dare not say what I think, even to you, Brace!'

There was a contraction of the young man's features, as an inkling of the meaning of his mother's hastily-spoken words flashed across his mind. Then, rising, he began to pace the room with impatient strides, for there was a sense of disappointment at his heart which he could not overcome; and in spite of his efforts, there seemed to be continually before him the sweet, timid face and the reclining figure that he had for a few minutes supported; while, as he pondered upon his mother's words, again piecing together her long narrative, it seemed to him that he was every minute being removed further and further from one who had made what in another case he would have called an impression upon a susceptible nature. It was as though each moment a deep, black gulf was opening wider and wider between them—a gulf that it would be impossible for him ever to pass. Then, as Mrs Norton watched him anxiously, he stood gazing from the window, telling himself that it was absurd to treat matters in such a light; that he had seen Isa Gernon but for a few minutes; that he had barely spoken to her; that she might be engaged to another; that she might be in disposition unamiable, and in tastes utterly opposed to his; that, in short, he was making an utter ass of himself. But, all the same, there were those two large, sad eyes ever before him, gazing reproachfully in his face from beyond that great gulf—ever widening more and more, more and more, till, impatiently stamping upon the floor, he made an angry effort to cast the ' folly ' from him, and went and knelt down by his mother's side.

'I am sorry, Brace,' she said, as her hand played, with all a proud mother's tenderness, amongst his fair, crisply-curling hair—' I am grieved that my words should have made so troublous an impression.'

'It is not that—it is not that ! There, what am I saying ? ' he exclaimed, with assumed cheerfulness. ' I've come home in high spirits, brimful of happiness, and ready to enjoy myself ; so, dear mother, don't let us trouble about the past—let it be buried.'

' Yes, better so—far better so ! ' exclaimed

Mrs Norton. 'For our sakes, Brace, never refer to it before your father in any wise; for those incidents were so many shoals in the way of his happiness; but, Brace, I set myself to try and make his life happy, and sometimes I cannot help thinking that I have succeeded.'

'Indeed, no happier home than this could ever have existed, I'm sure,' cried Brace, smiling in his mother's pleasant face. 'But,' he added, as he kissed her, laughing, 'it does seem hard that when you have cured a husband of a roving disposition, you should have a son turn out far worse.'

Mrs Norton smiled, but a grave, sad expression swept the next moment over her face.

'Save for his business transactions, Brace, that was your father's last long absence from me—for I suffered deeply then. I think that on his return from France, when he had had some arrangements made by which he gained time to pay off every demand, he saw how I had felt his absence, and made a resolve to leave me no more, and he has kept to that determination.'

'The mines nearly ruined him, then, in the first place ?' said Brace.

'Very nearly; but he had such faith in them that for five years we lived almost in poverty that we might pay off debts; when, as his last creditor was satisfied, your father's faith met with its reward, and ever since the mines have gone on increasing their returns year by year. But let us go to him now. You will be careful, though, Brace; you see now how necessary it is that not even a reference should be made to the bygone?'

'Yes—yes, mother—yes!' said Brace, with a troubled sigh; and they rose to leave the room, when, with the traces of his former emotion quite passed away, Captain Norton entered, looking inquiringly at mother and son, and then entering into conversation upon indifferent topics, as if nothing had happened.

CHAPTER VI.

RIGHT HONOURABLE.

'NOW, look here, Josh: it's of no use for you to come bothering me like this. Here have I been back from Italy only a few days, and you're down upon me like a leech— I mean like a hawk!'

'If your lordship had condescended to tell me that you were going abroad, and consulted me about the meeting of those little bills when they fell due, it would have been a different thing.'

The scene was a heavily-furnished room in

a fashionable London hotel, and the speakers were George Viscount Maudlaine, son and heir to the hampered estates and somewhat tarnished title of the Right Honourable Valentine, twentieth Earl of Chiltern; and Joshua Braham, Esq., solicitor, of Drury Chambers, St Alban's Place, Regent Street. The former, as he lounged back in his purple dressing-gown, appeared to be a tall, well-made young man, with a somewhat dreamy or tobacco-contemplative cast of countenance, more remarkable for bone, and the prominence of the well-known Chiltern features, than anything particularly definite; the latter was a gentleman, very smooth, very swarthy, possessing a ruddy and Eastern development of lip, aquiline of nose, hair short—black—spiky—of a texture, in short, that threatened, should a lock be sent for, to fly off in dangerous blinding showers of capillary stubble.

'You see, I don't recollect these sort of things,' said his lordship.

'Only when your lordship requires a fresh supply of money,' said Mr Braham, smiling like a shark, and rubbing his hands together so that his rings rattled.

'There, don't make a bother: sit down and have some breakfast, Braham,' said the younger man. 'These sort of things are so dooced unpleasant.'

'Unpleasant? There's nothing further from my thoughts, my lord, than making things unpleasant. I only came, after writing twice to remind your lordship that three bills, which fell due a month since, were all returned, and now lie in my hands, with interest and expenses attached. Unpleasant? Why, I give you my word, that Moss, or Peterson, or Barcohen, would have had your lordship arrested and in Bream's Buildings or Cursitor

Street days ago. But I don't do business like that. I only accommodate gentlemen of position, and then, in return, I expect to get the treatment one meets with from gentlemen of position.'

'You Israelitish hound!' muttered his lordship, 'I'd pitch you out of the window if I dared!'

'Did your lordship speak?' said the visitor, bending his head aside in an attitude of attention.

'Speak? No! Only I've such a confounded headache this morning, I'm not fit for business matters. Richmond last night with some friends.'

'Yes; I heard so,' said the visitor, softly. 'Mad'moiselle Duval was of the party, I think?'

'How the dooce did you know that?' exclaimed his lordship, uneasily.

'Oh! really I hardly know. It is one of
the troubles of position, my lord, that every
one hears of your movements.'

'I'll lay twenty to one that you've had
some hook-beaked, unshaven dog watching
me ever since I've been back!' exclaimed his
lordship, impetuously.

'He, he, he!' laughed the Jew. 'Your
lordship may have a headache, but you are
really most keen and business-like this morning.'

His lordship growled.

'*You* are,' he said, after a pause.

'Exactly so,' said the money-lender.
'And now, perhaps, your lordship will give
your attention to the matter in hand?'

'Well, I am attending!' grumbled his
lordship.

'Then, perhaps, your lordship will give me
a cheque on your banker for the total of the

bills, interest and expenses. Let me see,' continued the visitor, drawing a large bill-case from his pocket.

'There, keep that confounded thing out of my sight! My head aches quite badly enough without having that thrown in my teeth. Now, look here: I haven't fifty pounds at the banker's, and what there is I want for present expenses.'

'Then what does your lordship propose doing?'

'Nothing at all,' said his lordship sulkily.

'Does your lordship wish me to ask payment of the Earl, your father?'

'If you like,' said his lordship, with a grin; 'but while he has this fit of the gout on, I should not advise you to get within his reach. He holds to the fine old idea of his Norman ancestors, that knocking a Jew on the head was meritorious. But there! he won't pay— he can't, even if he felt ever so disposed. Now, look here, Braham : you must stick some more interest on, and renew the bills.'

' ' Renew, my lord ? ' exclaimed the money-lender, expressing with eyebrows and hands the greatest of surprise. ' Impossible ! I've renewed till I'm as sick of it as of your broken faith.'

' No, you're not ; so don't be a humbug ! ' said the Viscount. ' I'm not very sharp, I know ; but I'm keen enough to see through that. You've milked me pretty well, and worked me nicely with all your professional cant. I don't recollect how much I've had in cash—I did put it down on old envelopes, but they're lost—but I know that those pictures and the wines were horrible stuff; and one way and another you've made those bills grow till now they amount to—'

' Four thou—'

' There—there, that'll do ; I can't pay it,

so what's the good of bothering one about how much it is? I've got it down somewhere, I tell you, and perhaps I can find it when I want to know, and I don't now. Well, as I was going to say, you've made the bills grow to that size, now make them grow a little bigger.'

His lordship yawned, stretched himself, and then poured some pale brandy into a coffee-cup, before filling it with the rich fluid in the biggin.

'Totally impossible, my lord,' said the money-lender, rising. 'I'm very sorry, my lord, but I must set the law to work. I have, as you well know, always been most desirous of aiding you during pressing necessities; and when unable to help you myself, I have always introduced you to some one who would. But, to speak plainly, this trip of yours to Italy, without a word to me first—'

'Why, confound it all ! was I to come and ask you if I might go abroad?' exclaimed his lordship, furiously.

'Oh, dear me, no! Of course not, my lord ; but as I was saying, this trip to Italy looks so much like trying to bilk me, that I must, for my own sake—'

'And that of the gentleman in the City,' sneered his lordship.

'No, my lord, I don't do business with men in the City,' said the Jew, in injured tones ; 'and for my own sake alone I must take strenuous measures for the recovery of the debt.'

"'Tisn't a debt : it's only a money-lending affair,' growled his lordship.

'Well—well, we won't argue upon that point, my lord. The Sheriff of Middlesex has his ideas upon these matters—ideas in which I have implicit confidence.'

'Here, Braham; I say; come, no non-sense. Don't be a fool, you know. Don't be hard on a fellow because he's bilious and put out!' exclaimed his lordship, who, with the immediate prospect of a sponging-house before him, displayed an unwonted degree of per-turbation. 'But, I say, you can't—you know you can't do anything yet;' and his lordship's face brightened.

The Jew laughed.

'Your lordship forgets. Hyman has a little affair out against you, which will just work in well with mine. I shouldn't be sur-prised if some one is already waiting for you!'

'Oh! come, I say—you know; I can't stand this. You mustn't do anything, Braham; and you must stop Hyman, because I've come home—come over—come on pur-pose—that is, I have something good on my book.'

The money-lender watched him narrowly.

'Have indeed—matter of great importance —case of thousands, in fact—clear me of all my little unpleasantries.'

'Pooh!' ejaculated the money-lender, dropping the servile now that his client began to implore. 'Something on the Heath, or the Derby, or Oaks. I never knew one of your family yet with *nous* enough to do anything but lose. Now, look here, my lord: are you prepared to pay me four thousand three hun—'

'No; not a penny!' exclaimed his lordship, earnestly; 'but, look here, Braham,' he cried, catching his visitor by the button; 'I've got something in hand—I have indeed : not betting. Something safe and paying; but you must give me time, and let me have a few hundreds to carry on with.'

'Bah!' exclaimed the Jew fiercely, 'I'm

not going to be shilly-shallied with any more. Now, look here, my lord; I've given you time, and I've been patient. You've had documents served upon you; but even to the last I wouldn't be hard. I said to myself, I'll give him every chance; and I've done it; but you only turn round upon me like all the rest, friend as I've been to you. And now it has come to this—I've asked you to pay me, and you won't.'

' I can't, I tell you—'pon my word I can't,' exclaimed his lordship, following his visitor to the door, and pressing it back, as the other tried to get it open.

' Very well. Then I must have my pound of flesh!' said the Jew, with a bitter grin. ' Only, you see, my lord, we are wiser than our old ancestor, Shylock: we do not bargain for exact weight, and, to avoid the punishment awarded to the shedder of blood, we take the whole body. Your lordship weighs twelve stone, I should think ? '

' Fourteen stone,' said the Viscount, complacently.

' Plenty of weight, and to spare, then,' said the Jew, laughing.

' But you don't mean what you say, Braham ? ' said his lordship, anxiously.

' I never joke on money matters, my lord ; I've a couple of sheriff's officers and a cab across the road, my lord. If you will take the trouble to walk across to the window you can see them.'

Lord Maudlaine took a step across towards the window ; but he was back in an instant.

' But I say, Braham,' he exclaimed, ' this is getting serious—it is, indeed—and you mustn't, you know ; 'pon my word, you mustn't. Think of the scandal and the expense; and you won't do yourself any good, besides ruining me.'

'What do you mean by ruining you?' said the Jew, for the young nobleman's earnestness was such as no dread of a spunging-house, pure and simple, would have evoked—'what's in the wind?—what do you mean?'

'Well, I tell you, don't I? I've got something in hand—something good, you know.'

'What is it?'

There was a few minutes' silence as, driven to bay by his necessities, the scion of the not very noble house stood frowning and biting his lips.

'Just as you like,' said the Jew, coolly. 'I don't want you to tell me.' And he again tried to leave, but his lordship stayed him.

'Now, look here,' said the Jew again. 'I've always been a friend to you, Lord

Maudlaine, and I'll give you one more chance. What did you go to Italy for?'

There was no answer; and as his lordship stood with his back to the door, the visitor walked across to the window, as if to signal to one of the men waiting with the cab.

' Well, there,' exclaimed his lordship, ' to get out of your way.'

The Jew smiled.

' I expected as much. And now, why did you come back?'

' To—because— Well, there; it's connected with the—with the—the good thing I told you of.'

' Now, look here, young man,' said Abraham, without the ' A,' ' are we to be friends or enemies?'

' Friends, of course,' said the young nobleman, scowling.

' Then, look here: I must have perfect

openness. Just show me that this is something genuine—something worth waiting for, and I'll wait—of course, for a consideration.'

He waited for some response to his words, but none was forthcoming.

'I'm not going to be treated like this!' exclaimed the visitor, with mock anger. 'I'll soon—'

'There, there—stop, and I'll tell you all about it. It is worth waiting for.'

His lordship stopped short again, and his by no means intellectual countenance displayed strongly the shame and humiliation he felt.

'Well?' said the Jew.

'It's about a marriage—a matrimonial affair.'

The Jew looked at him as if he would read his every thought.

'Plenty of money?' he said, at last.

' One of the richest heiresses in England.'

' Are you sure of that ? ' said Braham ; ' or has some foreign countess got hold of you again ? '

' Sure ?   Yes ! ' cried Maudlaine, excitedly.   ' The father has been living out of England for years past at the rate of a couple of thousand a year, and his income's at least twenty.   All been increasing and piling up ever since.'

The Jew again looked piercingly at the young man ; but it was plain enough that the ability was not in him to invent this as a fiction upon the spur of the moment.

' Well,' said the interlocutor, ' go on. Have you any chance ? '

' Yes ; of course I have,' said Maudlaine.

' Father agreeable ? '

' Yes ! '

' Lady ? '

'Well, yes—pretty well; but that's all right, I tell you.'

'Meet them abroad?'

'Yes.'

'Have they come back to town?'

'To England—not town.'

'Humph!' ejaculated the visitor, still narrowly scanning his victim. 'And that's why you came back?'

'Of course.'

'Now, look here, Maudlaine,' said the Jew, fiercely, 'I'm not a man to be trifled with. I was your slave once, and you did not forget to show it. You are mine now, and you must not be surprised at my turn, now it has come, being brought strongly before your attention. But I'll be frank with you: I lend money for interest. Well and good: I'd rather wait and let you pay me that money and that interest than have to arrest you. I don't want to get a bad name amongst your class. Now I've not much confidence in you as to promises to pay; but I'll believe your word of honour. Is all this true?'

'On my word of honour, yes!' said Maudlaine, angrily.

'Who is the lady, then?'

The Viscount flushed deeply, bit his lips, and was silent; for to answer this question seemed to him too great a humiliation.

'Who is the lady?' was asked again.

There was no answer.

'I suppose you don't want my help, then?' said the Jew. 'Just as you like. Prove to me that this is worth my while to wait—say six or twelve months—and I'll lend you a few hundreds to go on with. But, there, I'm not anxious; just as you like. Shall I call up the men?'

'Confound you, no!' exclaimed the young

man, angrily. 'She is the daughter of a wealthy baronet, of Lincolnshire. Now are you satisfied?'

'No,' said the Jew, taking out pencil and pocket-book; 'I want his name.'

'Good old family,' said the Viscount, hastily. 'Only child. I am invited down there, and the baronet is quite willing. Will that do?'

'Name—name—name!' exclaimed the creditor, impatiently.

'Sir Murray Gernon. There, then!' cried the young man, furiously.

'Sir Murray Gernon,' said the Jew, quietly, as he tapped his teeth with his large gold pencil-case—'Sir Murray Gernon. Ah! let me see; there was a screw loose there, if I recollect right, years ago. Rich family, though—very. Young lady's mamma bolted, I think; but that don't matter to you. Yes,

that will do, Viscount—that will do. I think
I'll wait.'

'And you will advance me what I require?' said his lordship, eagerly, forgetting
all humiliation in his brightened prospects.

'In reason, yes,' said the Jew, with a mocking smile once more overspreading his face;
'but I shall not do it for nothing, my Lord
Viscount Maudlaine—I shall not do it for
nothing.'

'No,' muttered the young man, 'I know
that.'

'It's quite possible that I may go so far as
to make my own terms,' said the Jew, with a
grin. 'But I'll leave you, now, to think over
the matter; and if you want any little help, of
course you'll come to my chambers, where we
can renew one of the bills'

'Confound the bills!' cried the young

man, angrily ; ' I must have a cheque for some hard cash to go on with.'

' Very good. Come to me, then, my lord,' said the Jew, all suavity once more. ' Excuse me for hurrying away, but it is for your sake. It is not seemly to have Sheriffs' officers waiting opposite to an hotel. Good morning, my lord ! '

' Good morning ! ' said the Viscount, sulkily.

' You shall fly a little longer, my fine bird —just a little longer ! ' said Mr Joshua Braham, as he went out ; ' but it shall be just as long as I like, and with a string tied to your leg—a string, my fine fellow, of which I hold the end ! '

CHAPTER VII.

IN PERIL.

'IT is of no use,' said Brace Norton, one day, when he had been home about a month, ' I can't fight against fate. I vowed that I'd think no more about her, and I've thought about nothing else ever since. I go out very seldom, but when I do, I always seem to meet her. I've heard a good deal of milk-and-sugar talk about love ; and if this is what is called love, all I can say is that it's worse than mast-heading. I can't help it—I can't keep free of it ! What in the world did I get looking at her for, as I did, that day coming home ? ¦Brace Norton—Brace Norton, I'm afraid that you are a great ass ! '

He sat thinking for awhile, trying to be light-hearted, and to sweep his troubles away, but he soon owned to himself that it was no laughing matter.

' Heaven help me ! ' he groaned, ' for a miserable, unhappy wretch—one who seems fated to make those about him suffer ! It seems almost as if I were to endure the same torments as my poor father, without the allevi- ation of some other gentle hand to heal my wounds. Wounds ! Pooh ! stuff ! What romantic twaddle I am talking ! It is time I was off back to sea. But, there, I've fought against it, all for their sakes, till it has been enough to drive me mad. I suppose men were meant to be butterflies, and to burn their wings in the light of some particular star ; so the sooner I get mine singed off, and get on board ship, the better. There's no romance there. Anything's better than this state of torment. Here am I, making myself disagreeable to the best of fathers and the tenderest of mothers ; and because things run in a rut different from that which suits me, I go sulking about like a spoiled child in love with a jam-pot ; and after making everybody miserable at home, go sneaking and wandering about after the fashion of a confounded tramp poaching somebody's goslings. I expect I shall be locked up one of these days. Seriously, though, I wish I had not come back,' he said, dreamily ; 'I wish that a reconciliation were possible ; I wish I had never seen her ; I wish—I wish—There, what is the good of wishing ? What a wretched life this is, and how things do contrive to get in a state of tangle ! I don't think I ever tried to meet her, and yet how often, day after day, we seem to encounter! Even the thought of the old past sorrows seems to bring her closer and closer. Why, then, should not this be the means of bringing old sorrows to an end, and linking together the two families?'

Brace Norton brought his ponderings to a close, as, bit by bit, he recalled the past; and then he groaned in spirit, as his reason told him how impossible was a reconciliation.

'I must dismiss it all,' he at last said, bitterly. 'They have had their sufferings; I will not be so cowardly as to shrink from mine. I'll take an interest in the governor's pursuits; and here goes to begin. I'll run over to the Marsh, and see where they are pegging out the drain; but I may as well take a gun, and see if I cannot bag a couple or two of ducks.'

Brace Norton's reverie had been in his

own room ; and with this determination fresh upon him, he walked, cheery of aspect, into the room where Captain and Mrs Norton had been discussing the unsatisfactory turn matters had taken, when the young man's bright look, and apparently buoyant spirits, came upon them like a burst of sunshine.

' Gun ? Yes, my dear boy ! ' exclaimed the Captain, delighted at the change that seemed to have come over his son. ' Here you are,' he said, opening a case—'everything to your hand. You'll be back to dinner ? '

' Ay, ay, sir ! ' cried Brace, strengthened in his resolve, on seeing the pleasure his high spirits seemed to impart to his elders. ' I am going to see where they are marking out the drain.'

' To be sure. Quite right, Brace—quite right. I should like, above all things, to go with you.'

'Well, why not?' said Brace, heartily.

Captain Norton smiled, and shook his head, as he pointed to his writing-table, covered with correspondence.

'Too much engaged, my boy—too many letters to write. I'll go over with you one day, though, if you will.'

'To be sure,' said Brace.

And then he saluted his mother, who held his hands tightly, as if unwilling to part from him, as she gazed fondly in his face. Then having secured the gun and ammunition, he started off, with a bold, elastic step, apparently as free from care as if no cloud had crossed his young career.

He had not gone far before again and again came the longing desire to sit down beneath some shady tree, and picture the soft sweet face that his heart whispered him he loved—the face that seemed to be so impressed upon his brain, that, sleeping or waking, asked for or. uncalled, it was always there vividly before his gaze ; though, beyond a distant salute and its response, since the day of the accident, he had never held the slightest intercourse with Isa Gernon. He might have laughed at another for being so impressionable ; but, none the less, he felt himself to be greatly moved, and hour by hour he felt that the task he had imposed upon himself was greater than he could ever expect to master.

But that day Brace would not yield to the sweet temptation, striving manfully and trying hard to tire himself out. He visited the portions of the great marsh where arrangements were being made for forming the drain ; he tramped to and fro over the boggy land with his gun, hour after hour ; and at last, utterly weary, he entered the pine-wood on the marsh edge, having unwittingly wandered to the spot where, years before, his father had, in his wild despair, so nearly cast away his life.

It was with a sigh of satisfaction that he leaned his gun against a tree, and seated himself upon the fallen trunk of a large fir; for there was something soothing to his feelings in the solemn silence of this vast nature-temple. There was a soft, warm glow cast aslant amidst the tall smooth pillars by the descending sun, and but for the soft sigh of a gentle gale, and the sharply-repeated tap of the woodpecker sounded at intervals, there was nothing to break the stillness, which to another might have seemed oppressive.

And now, with a fierce rush, the dammed-back thoughts made at him. Now was the time for reverie—here in this solitary place. But no—he would not weakly succumb. It was not to be: he had made a resolution, and he would keep it. He boldly set himself to fight with a power stronger than himself, blindly thinking that he might succeed.

How had he succeeded with his gun?

He smiled as he looked at the result of his many hours' tramp—one solitary teal; and then for a few moments he was dwelling musingly upon the great subject that had filled his mind during the past month, but only to dismiss it angrily. He sighed, though, the next moment, and the soft breeze bore away the word 'Isa'; and then romance faded as Brace sought solace in the small case he drew from his pocket, from which he selected a very foreign-looking cigar, lit it, and leaning back, began to emit cloud after cloud of thin blue vapour, till the tobacco roll was smoked to the very end, when Brace rose, calm and refreshed, ready to journey homeward.

'A sonnet to his mistress's eyebrow,' said Brace, as he moved over the pine-needles. 'Not so bad as that, though, after all.'

He had not proceeded a dozen yards, though, before he remembered that he had left his gun behind, leaning against a tree; and hurrying back, he was in the act of taking it, when a distant cry came floating through the trees.

'Hullo!' exclaimed Brace, as he caught up his gun. 'Curlew? No, it was not a curlew; but I've grown so used to the wail of the sea birds, that I don't know those of my native place. Ha! there it is again.'

For once more the cry came ringing faintly by—a long, low, prolonged scream, as of some one in peril; when, roused by the exciting promise of adventure, he ran swiftly in the direction from whence the cry seemed to have come.

In a few minutes he was at the edge of the grove, gazing over the open marsh, to see nothing ; when, fancying that he must have come in the wrong direction, he stood listening intently for another cry.

A full minute elapsed—a minute during which he could hear his heart beating heavily —and then once more came the loud wail, plainly enough now, and forming the appealing word that goes home to every heart :

' Help ! '

The next moment Brace Norton was dashing over the treacherous bog, leaping from tuft to tuft of the silky cotton rush, avoiding verdant patches of moss, which concealed watery, muddy pools, and finding foothold where the heather grew thickly. Twice he sank in to his knees, but he dashed on to where, at the distance of some three or four hundred yards from the pine-wood, he had made out a figure struggling in one of the profound holes filled with deep amber-coloured water, while, as he rushed on, at times floundering and splashing in the soft peat, it seemed to him that his aid would arrive too late.

A light muslin dress, a portion of which, still undrenched, buoyed up its wearer; a little straw hat, fallen off to float on the dark waters; a pale, upturned, agonized face; long clusters of hair rippling with the troubled element; and two dark, wild, appealing eyes, seeming to ask his aid. Brace Norton saw all this in the few moments ere he reached the side of the pit; but as he recognized the features, a cry of anguish tore from his heart, as, falling heavily, it was some little time before he could regain his feet. Then, with a rush and a plunge, he sent the water foaming in great waves to the green and deceptive sides of the moor-pit, still trembling with the weight that had lately passed over them. Another minute, and with the energy of a stout swimmer he had forced himself through the dozen yards of water that intervened, to reach at and grasp an arm, just as the water was bubbling up above a fair, white forehead, and playing amidst the long tresses floating around. Another instant, and Brace's arm was supporting the drowning girl, as he swam stoutly towards the side.

The distance was short, but unfortunately the side he reached was but a semi-fluid collection of bog vegetation, half floating upon the water, and which broke away from the arm he threw over it again and again.

He swam off after two or three essays, laboriously now, with his burden, to another part of the pool, but that was worse; the moss breaking away at a touch. He looked towards

the other side, some forty yards away, but
with his precious load he dared not try to
swim the distance.

To make matters worse, the sides of the
pool were not perpendicular, but the loose
vegetation grew out a couple of feet or so over
the water, as if, in the course of years, to cover
it with the treacherous green carpet, spread in
so many other places over deep black pits;
and thus any attempt to gain foothold and
climb out was vain; while, for aught he could
tell, the pool might have been fifty feet deep
beneath his feet.

To stay where he was seemed impossible,
so, swimming a few yards, he made to where
—partly to rest, partly to think upon the best
plan of procedure—he could tightly grasp a
tuft of rushes with his disengaged hand. But
even this was no safeguard, for he could feel
that a very slight effort would be required to

draw the tuft from its hold. And now, for the first time, he turned to gaze earnestly in the pallid face so close to his, to find the eyes dilate and horror-stricken, while two little hands were tightly clasped round his neck.

'Do not be alarmed, Miss Gernon,' he whispered, his heart throbbing almost painfully the while. 'Give me a few moments to recover breath, and then I will draw you ashore —or rather,' he said, with an encouraging smile, 'on to this treacherous moss.'

The smile was intended to chase away the dread of there being imminent danger, and it had its effect.

'I am not very—very much frightened,' she half sobbed, though, unable to conceal her agitation, she clung to him tightly. 'I was picking marsh flowers when the rushes suddenly gave way beneath my feet.'

'The place is very dangerous,' said Brace;

and then, in an earnest voice—'Thank Heaven, though, that I was so near at hand.'

He paused for a few moments to gaze in her face, and in that brief space of time danger—the water—all was forgotten as their eyes met, for hers to fall directly before his loving, earnest look. For there, in spite of what he had said, in great peril, but with her heart beating against his, so that he could feel its pulsations, all Brace Norton's resolutions faded away; and for a moment he thought of how sweet it would be to die thus—to loose his hold of the rushes, to clasp his other arm round her, and then, with an end to all the sorrow and heart-burning of this life, with her clinging to him as she might never cling again, to let the water close above their heads, and then—

'What a romantic fool I am,' thought Brace. 'Here, a month ago, I thought life one of the jolliest things in the world; and now I'm thinking in this love-sick, unhealthy, French, charcoal-and-brimstone style of suicide.'

The reaction gave his mind tone; for directly after, Brace Norton was thinking how sweet it would be to live, perhaps earning Isa Gernon's love as well as her gratitude, for saving her sweet life; and with a flush upon his cheek for his weak thoughts, Brace nerved himself for the effort he was about to make.

With his right hand tightly clutching the rush tuft, he tried to thrust his feet into the bank beneath; but in spite of a tremendous and exhausting effort, the sole result was, that the portion of the edge he clung to came away in his hand, and with the plunge, they were the next instant both beneath the water. A few vigorous strokes, though, and Brace was once more at the side with the half-fainting girl well supported, as a bunch of rushes once more supplied him with a hold for his clinging fingers.

'Oh, pray—pray save me!' murmured Isa, faintly, as a cold chill shot through her, and her pale face grew almost ghastly.

'With Heaven's help I will!' exclaimed Brace, thickly, 'or I'll die with you!'

The words seemed to be forced from his lips by his strong emotion, and he could perceive that she heard them. He knew, too, that she had recognized him at the first. The words took their impassioned tone, in spite of himself; and he repented, as he saw a faint flush of colour—it might have been from indignation—rise to her cheeks.

But there was no time for dallying with thoughts of such engendering, for he knew that every moment only robbed him of so much power, and he prepared for another effort.

'Hold me tightly,' he said. 'Don't be afraid; only let me have both hands at liberty, so that I may be able to drag myself out.'

She did as he wished, and he struggled hard; but the weight clinging to him frustrated every effort, and after five minutes' vain expenditure of strength, Brace had great difficulty in finding firm hold for his grasp; while his heart sank, as he found that what at first had seemed but a trifling mishap, and an opportunity for displaying his knight-errantry, now began to loom forth in proportions ominous to them both.

He looked in every direction now, where the tall reeds did not shut out the view, for he was beginning to mistrust his own power; but there was not a soul within sight. And now, for the first time, he raised his voice, to cry loudly for help—despairingly, though, for he could not think it possible that aid could be near. He called again and again; but his voice seemed to be lost in the vast space, and sounded faint, adding to the chill of despair creeping to his heart; till, rousing himself, after regaining his breath, he adopted the plan that he should have tried at first.

'Miss Gernon!—Isa! For Heaven's sake, speak!' he cried, earnestly, as he gazed at the half-closed eyes and the drooping head. 'Try and rouse yourself for one more effort!'

She heard his words, and her eyes unclosed, and rested upon his for an instant.

'That's right!' he cried, joyfully. 'Now, quick! loose your hold of me! Don't cling, but take hold here of these reeds where my hand is, and hold there tightly for a few moments. I can, then, perhaps, get out, and draw you after me: I am quite powerless here. Can you hold on for half a minute?'

Isa's pale lips parted, but no audible words came. She obeyed him, though, and he guided her cold, white hand to the sharp-edged leaves.

'Now, then, be brave! Keep a good heart, for the sake of all who love you!' he whispered; and loosing his hold, he paused for an instant or two, to find that she was striving gallantly to obey him. 'Only a few moments!' he cried; and then, summoning all his strength, he left her, and by means of a desperate effort fought and plunged his way through the now clinging—now yielding mass, till—how he could not tell—he forced his way on, to lie panting, at full length, amongst the rushes. The next moment a cry of despair burst from his breast; for, as he drew himself along to where Isa Gernon clung, he saw that the tuft of reeds, disturbed by his frantic efforts, were parting from the edge, and directly after the poor girl's head sank again beneath the black water.

A rush—a plunge—a fierce struggle, and Brace was nearly free of the mosses and water-weeds ; but now they seemed to cling round him more than ever, hampering his efforts, and minutes seemed to have elapsed before he had shaken himself clear, and dived down into the depths of the pool, forcing his way lower and lower till half strangled, when, rising to the surface, he drew a long, gasping breath, and then again plunged down.

It was well for Brace Norton that many a time he had swum and dived for sport in far off tropic waters, till he had gained a mastery over the element which now stood him in good stead ; for at this second plunge far down into the black depths his hand came in contact with Isa Gernon's long, flowing hair, and the next instant he had risen to the surface and held her at the pool edge, with her lips well above water, he clinging the while to the reeds, as, with all the force he could muster from his panting breast, he once more shouted hoarsely for help.

CHAPTER VIII.

RESCUE.

'I'VE done my part,' muttered Brace Norton, as, in spite of the despair of the moment, he yielded to his feelings, kissing fondly again and again the cold pale lips of the insensible girl. 'I can do no more. Help must come from elsewhere, or— No, I will not give up, if only for her sake.' And once more he hoarsely shouted for the help that he could not think would come.

The loosening of one arm so that the burden might glide from him—a strong effort, and he could once more have been amongst the reeds and mosses ; but it would have been like leaving the brighter portion of his life to death ; and his eyes glared fiercely as he clutched the fair, slight figure more tightly to his breast. It was like fighting against a cruel temptation, one which whispered to him of the brightness of his young life that he was casting away for the sake of an enemy's daughter—of his home, and his weeping mother.

The temptation was strong, but he could not play the coward's part ; and he held Isa to him more and more closely, gloating over the soft, regular features, as, with a pang hard to bear, he told himself the next moment that, even if help came, it would arrive too late.

That same afternoon Sir Murray Gernon strode out into the pleasure-grounds, thoughtfully crossed the lawn, avoiding, as it were,

more by instinct than care, the various flower-
beds, till he roused himself, with a start, on
finding that he was standing at the very edge
of the lake, gazing down into its deep waters,
as if they possessed for him some horrible fas-
cination.

He stood there for full ten minutes, his
brow corrugated, his eyes staring, and his teeth
clenched firmly upon his lower lip. Then with
an effort he seemed to drag himself, shuddering,
away, to walk slowly muttering to himself.

Fifty yards of winding amidst flower-beds
and shrubs, and Sir Murray came suddenly
upon Lord Maudlaine, his guest, seated upon
a garden-chair, a half-smoked cigar in one
hand, a newspaper at his feet, his mouth half
open, and his aristocratic head resting upon
his open palm.

It is quite possible that Sir Murray Gernon
might have passed his visitor, who had already

been for some days at the Castle, but for the fact that certain strange sounds arrested his attention. Had these sounds procceded from Alexander M'Cray, there would have been no difficulty about the matter, and one would have immediately said that the ex-gardener was snoring loudly; but when a nobleman is concerned, a diffidence—an unwillingness is felt to use such a term. However, Lord Maudlaine was loudly trumpeting forth the announcement that he was devoting a spare hour to the service of Morpheus, and Sir Murray Gernon, hearing those sounds, was attracted thereby.

'You here, Maudlaine?' exclaimed Sir Murray.

'Eh?' Why, what the deuce— Dear me! I suppose I was dozing,' said his lord-ship, lifting himself up a bit at a time, as he indulged in a most unmistakable yawn.

'Not with Isa?' said Sir Murray. 'I thought you went out with her?'

'Ya-as—ya-as! no question of a doubt about it, I did,' drawled the Viscount; 'and I've just been dreaming that I was boating with her on the lake—not your fish-pond here, but Como—same as we did before we came away.'

'But you went out walking with her?' said Sir Murray, anxiously.

'Ya-as. Not a question of a doubt about it! I did go out and walked a little way with her.'

'Did she turn back, then?'

'N-n-no!' said the Viscount; 'point of fact, she as good as told me she didn't want me, and went on by herself.'

'My dear Maudlaine,' said Sir Murray, smiling, as he clapped his guest upon the shoulder, 'I'm afraid that you are not half a lady's man. It is a fine thing for you that you have no rival in the field.'

'Ya-as—just so—no doubt about that,' said his lordship laughing. 'But a—a I began talking to her on indifferent subjects, and, point of fact, she didn't seem to like indifferent subjects—seemed as if I bothered her, you know, and of course I didn't want to do that; so seeing, as you say, that there was no one else in the field—regular walk over the course, you know—I didn't bother her nor myself either. We're getting on very nicely, though, Sir Murray—very nicely indeed. No question about that.'

'I'm glad to hear it,' said Sir Murray, dryly.

'Ya-as; beginning to understand one another's idio—what is it?—syncracies, don't you call it? I think Isa likes me.'

'Oh! yes, of course—of course!' said Sir

Murray. 'By the way, Maudlaine,' he continued, taking the young man's arm and walking slowly with him down a path, 'I hope you will be particular about the place; for I dare say I shall give it up to you young folks. I mean to be pretty stringent, though, I can assure you: I won't have a tree touched—no timber felled; there is none too much now. I should not like the lake drained either: I should particularly object to that. It might be said,' continued Sir Murray, hastily, 'that it made the place damp; but I don't think it —I don't think it.'

'Wouldn't dream of doing anything distasteful, of course,' said the Viscount. 'Always be glad of your advice, of course, if I had any ideas of improving anything. By the way, though, Gernon, she's mad after botany.'

'She? Who is?' said Sir Murray, starting.

'She is—Isa, you know. I shall have to work it up, for she don't seem to like my not being able to enter into the names of weeds with her. Not a weedy man myself, you know, eh? Ha, ha, ha!' And he laughed at what he intended for a joke.

'Was she botanizing to-day?' said Sir Murray, huskily.

'Ya-a-as! Said it was her mother's favourite pursuit, though I don't know why she should like it for that reason, eh?'

'Who told her that absurd nonsense?' exclaimed Sir Murray, angrily.

'Well, she did tell me,' said the lover; 'but, a—a—really, you know, I can't recollect. Don't particularly want to know, I suppose?'

'Oh no—oh no!' exclaimed Sir Murray, impatiently. 'But this place, Maudlaine— I should like it kept as it is: the timber, you know; and you would not drain the lake?'

'Oh no! of course not. But, I say, you know, I—a—a—a suppose it will be all right?'

'Right—all right?' said Sir Murray, whose face wore a cadaverous hue. 'What do you mean by all right?'

'Well, you know, I mean about Isa. I haven't said anything pointed to her yet, though we two have made it all right. She won't refuse me, eh?'

'Refuse? No: absurd!'

'Well, I don't know so much about that. I get thinking sometimes that she ain't so very far gone with me. Snubs me, you know, —turns huffy, and that sort of thing.'

'My dear Maudlaine,' said Sir Murray, with a sneering laugh, which there was no need of the other interpreting, 'you are too timid—too diffident for a man of your years.'

'Well, I don't know,' said his lordship, 'I don't think I am; but she's a style of woman I'm not used to. Don't seem dazzled, and all that sort of thing, you know. Some women would be ready to jump out of their skins to be a viscountess, and by-and-by an earl's wife; but she don't—not a bit—not that sort of woman; and if I never said a word about it, I don't believe that she would, even if I went on visiting here for years.'

'Most likely not,' said Sir Murray, dryly; 'but you see that it is as I say—you are too timid—too diffident.'

'I say, though, you know,' said his lordship, 'was her mother that style of woman—quiet and fond of weed-hunting—botany, you know?'

'You will oblige me greatly by not referring to the late Lady Gernon,' said Sir Murray, stiffly.

'Oh, beg pardon, you know. No offence meant.'

'It is granted,' said Sir Murray; and then, in a different tone : 'There goes the dressing-bell.'

The gentlemen strolled up in silence to the entrance, where the major-domo—Mr Alexander M'Cray—who seemed to rule supreme at Merland, now stood waiting the arrival of his master.

'I'm thinking, Sir Mooray,' he said deferentially, 'that ye'd like a pony-carriage sent to meet my young lady.'

'What—has she not returned?' said Sir Murray, anxiously.

'Nay, Sir Mooray, not yet awhile, and I should hae sent wi'oot saying a word, but that I thocht my laird here would tell us which road she gaed.'

'Towards the waste—the snipe ground,

you know,' said his lordship, on being appealed to.

'Send at once, M'Cray. No: go yourself,' said Sir Murray.

'I'll go with him,' said his lordship, who now seemed about wakening to the fact that he had grossly neglected his intended; and five minutes after the old Scot was driving briskly towards the village.

'Ye dinna ought to have left her, my laird,' said M'Cray, sturdily. 'She's ower young to be left all alone.'

'What? Were you speaking to me?' said his lordship, haughtily.

'Ay, that I was,' said M'Cray. 'Ye mauna mind me, my laird, for I'm a'most like her foster-fairther, and nursed her on my knee mony's the time.'

His lordship did not condescend to answer, and the lanes were traversed at a good rattling pace ; but though M'Cray pulled up from time to time to make inquiries, the only news he learned was that Miss Gernon had been seen to go towards the marsh, but not to return ; while one cottager volunteered the information that young Squire Norton, the sailor, went that way too in the morning time, and that neither of them had been seen to come back.

This news had no effect upon Lord George Maudlaine, but a close observer would have seen that the wrinkles upon Alexander M'Cray's brow grew a little more deeply marked.

' He's a douce laddie,' muttered M'Cray, as he drove on, ' and warth a score sic birkies as this one ; but it was ill-luck his meeting as they did that day, and it winna do—it winna do ! We shall be having sair wark yet, I'm afraid. They're kittlecattle these women-kind, and I nearly suffered shipwreck with them mysel'.'

' There's no one here,' said his lordship, now condescending to speak, as they drove to where the road faded away into a faint track, which, in its turn, led to the pine-grove.

' We'll get doon and hopple the ponies, my laird, and walk on to the pine-wood. My young leddie may be in there.'

' Confound his barbarous tongue ! Why don't he speak English ? ' muttered the Viscount. ' I don't understand one-half he says.'

But M'Cray's acts were plain enough, even if his words were obscure ; and, descending, he secured the ponies, and was about to start towards the wood, already looking black and gloomy, when one of Brace Norton's cries for help smote his ear.

' Gude save me ! Hearken to that, noo ! ' cried M'Cray, excitedly.

'Only a marsh bird,' said his lordship, contemptuously.

'Gude save us! Come alang; that's a soul in sair peril, my laird.' And starting in the direction of the cry, as fast as the treacherous nature of the ground would allow, M'Cray soon came in sight of that which made him redouble his pace.

'Here! Help, here!' cried a voice from behind. 'I'm sinking!' When, with a glance over his shoulder, M'Cray saw that his companion was already above his knees in a soft place.

'Deil help ye—ye ill-far'ed, handle-named loon!' muttered M'Cray, fiercely. 'Why couldna ye walk like a Christian, and not get in that way? I've ither work in hand.'

Then hastening on, he stepped from tuft to tuft, with an agility not to have been expected in a man of his years, till well within reach of words :

'Haud oup, then,' he cried—'haud oup, my bra'e laddie, I'm with ye. There!' he cried, as he threw himself at full length upon the yielding moss, and reached to where, ghastly of face, Brace still clung, and held up his charge—'there! I ha'e yer hand. Loose the rushes, and grip it weel—grip it weel.'

'Her first—take her first,' sobbed Brace, hoarsely.

'That I will!' cried M'Cray, working himself forward. 'Gude save us, though, it's sair wet work here, and I'm a deal heavier than I thocht. Noo I ha'e her, and she's leet as swansdoon aifter a'. The puir bairn, I ha'e her safe, but she's half dead. Lie there, my pretty, while I pu' out the laddie. Noo, my laddie; that's reet—that's reet; the ither hand. Noo again. Gude—gude! another pu'.

Hech ! laddie, mind, or I shall be in wi' ye.
Noo then, anither pu' ! That's weel ! I ha'e
ye noo. Puir lad, ye're cauld indeed, but
ye're safe, and reet too, so lie there while I
tak' the lassic.'

In effect, with the exertion of his great
strength, M'Cray, broad-shouldered and iron
muscled, had drawn both Isa and Brace from
what had so nearly been a watery grave, but
not without danger to himself. Twice over
the moss gave way with the stress placed upon
it ; but at last he had both lying safe beside
him, and not before it was time, for Brace was
completely exhausted.

'Let me carry her,' said Brace, hoarsely,
as he staggered to his feet ; but only to sink
down again, his numbed limbs refusing their
office.

'Ye're a bra'e laddie,' said the Scot ; 'but
your sperrit's stronger than your power. I'll

carry the lassie to the carriage, and be back for you in a minute.'

'Never mind me,' groaned Brace. 'I'm only cold. For Heaven's sake drive off with her, for she is nearly dead with her long immersion.'

But before Brace's words were well uttered, M'Cray was sturdily trudging over the sinking way with his dripping burden, which he placed in the pony carriage, covered with a rug, and then returned to help the young man, who was crawling towards him.

'Bra'e laddie, ye air,' muttered M'Cray. 'Ye found and savit her, I ken, and noo, half dead yersel', ready to help, while that loon stands stoock there shouting for succour, and afraid to move. Here, hi! my laird, move yersel', man, and, Gude sake, get out of that!'

'Here, give me your hand, my good

fellow,' cried his lordship : 'I'm in a dangerous spot.'

M'Cray growled fiercely as he went first and helped Brace to the chaise. Then turning back, he reached out the asked-for hand to extricate his lordship, but in so rough a manner that he nearly brought him into a horizontal position.

'Why, ye micht ha'e done that yersel', my laird,' said M'Cray, angrily. 'And noo I must leave ye, and hurry hame wi' those two puir bairns.'

His lordship began to offer expostulations as he began to scuffle out of the bog, but it was to deaf ears, for M'Cray had run back, and before the noble suitor was on *terra firma* the ponies were unloosed and being made to gallop over the rough roadway.

'They'll be dead wi' cauld before I can get them to the Castle,' muttered M'Cray, as he held Isa in his arm, and rattled the reins with the other, so that the ponies plunged along furiously. 'Puir bairns—puir bairns!'

M'Cray's words were muttered, but Brace caught their meaning.

'Drive to the Hall,' he said, hoarsely; 'it is quite a couple of miles nearer.'

'Gude sake! I might just as weel commit a murder,' muttered the Scot. 'But I shall commit one if I dinna get house-room for the lassie directly. I'll e'en do as he says, if I dee for it. Get on wi' ye!' he roared to the ponies, already speeding along like the wind, when, being no inexpert Jehu, he kept them at a sharp gallop, till a few minutes after, when he drew them up on their haunches at the door of Merland Hall.

END OF VOL. II.

JOHN CHILDS AND SON, PRINTERS.